THE LONG-AWAITED ARREST OF LONG ISLAND SERIAL KILLER REX HEUERMANN ~ PAST "ADMINISTRATION" TO BLAME

by Robert Banfelder

BB

~

Broadwater Books
Riverhead, New York

Broadwater Books
141 Riverside Drive
Riverhead, New York 11901

ISBN: 978-1-7326025-1-9

Printed in the United States of America
10 9 8 7 6 5 4 3 2 1

DEDICATION

This nonfictional accounting is dedicated to Donna Derasmo, whose invaluable assistance went into formatting narrative, researching, designing graphics, along with endless editing. These elements are among the many tasks Donna has taken on in bringing this eighteenth work of prose to full fruition. Donna has always been by my side, encouraging me to fulfill my dreams as a writer of both fiction and nonfiction. She will always have my undying love.

BOOKS BY ROBERT BANFELDER

FICTION

Trilogy:

Dicky, Richard, and I

The Signing

The Triumvirate

Tetralogy:

[A Justin Barnes Four-Book Series]

The Author
Award Winner for Best Suspense Novel from NewBookReviews

The Teacher
Award Winner for Best Suspense Novel from NewBookReviews

Knots

The Good Samaritans

FICTIONAL/FACTUAL ACCOUNTINGS

Trace Evidence
Inspired by and based on the Robert Shulman serial killer trial, Riverhead, Long Island, New York

Battered
Inspired by and based on the murder trial of Sylvia Flynn, Brick Township, New Jersey

NOUVEAU JOURNALISM
An admixture of Fact ~ Fiction ~ Supposition

The Long Island Serial Killer Murders ~ Gilgo Beach and Beyond
A well-received fictional/nonfictional account of one of the most notorious serial cases of our time ~ books purchased in the United States, Canada, United Kingdom, Germany

Snuff Stuff
Gilgo Beach/Oak Beach/Manorville/Atlantic City Serial Killer Murders
Sequel to *The Long Island Serial Killer Murders ~ Gilgo Beach and Beyond*

NONFICTION

The Essential Guide to Writing Well and Getting Published with Bonus Feature: *Making Decent Dollars Writing Plus Little-Known Reward-Reaping Benefits*

The Fishing Smart Anywhere Handbook for Salt Water & Fresh Water
Spin Casting, Baitcasting, Fly Casting ~ Lethal Lures & Live Baits ~ Kayaking/Canoeing ~ Seafood Recipes ~ Smoking Fish

The North American Hunting Smart Handbook with Bonus Feature:
Hunting Africa's Five Most Dangerous Game Animals

Bull's Eye! The Smart Bowhunter's Handbook with Bonus Feature:
Bowfishing on a Budget

On Your Way to Gourmet Cooking
A Unique Guide for both the Beginner and Veteran Cook ~ 50 Outstanding Recipes

Gourmet Cooking with Confidence
A Unique Guide for the Beginner and Veteran Chef
Plus Budget-Friendly Tools & Equipment for Making Life Easier in the Kitchen

INTRODUCTION

As the reader peruses these pages, he or she will note pertinent information regarding accused serial killer Rex Heuermann, disgraced former Suffolk County Chief of Police James Burke, disgraced former Suffolk County District Attorney Thomas Spota, and his disgraced former Anti-corruption Bureau Chief Christopher McPartland. The four will be presented intermittently throughout the book. This approach will avoid bogging the reader down with too much information at one time as there is much to cover within these pages. Also, specifically related timetables referencing these major characters as well as the murder victims in lieu of lengthy prose will expedite the writing process. For example, trying to encapsulate all relevant information from a 598-page book titled *A Criminal Injustice* by Richard Firstman and Jay Salpeter referencing the Marty Tankleff murder case is unnecessary when a minimal bulleted synopsis will succinctly suffice in drawing out pertinent data I want to present. Breaking up a specific incident into palatable sections avoids ennui, delivering powerful prose in small doses rather than in prolific mouthfuls of minutiae.

The culture of corruption and incompetence referencing Suffolk County law enforcement is concisely covered between the years 1979–2022. This period particularly includes a brief history of the Johnny Pius murder case; the Seymour/Arlene Tankleff murders, the seventeen-year false imprisonment of their adopted son, Marty Tankleff, the misdirection and cover-up by detectives James McCready and Norman Rein, the purported accomplices and/or co-conspirators to those murders: Jerry Steuerman, Joseph Creedon, Peter Kent, Glenn Harris; and the Rex Heuermann Gilgo Beach murder case—victims: Megan Waterman, Melissa Barthelemy, Amber Lynn Costello, and possibly Maureen Brainard-Barnes.

One cannot begin to understand the culture of corruption in Suffolk County—featuring two of its major players, a young Jimmy Burke and an aspiring middle-aged prosecutor, Thomas Spota—until one goes back in time to the late 70s. The pair went on to become the infamous Suffolk County's chief of police and district attorney, respectively. The duo thwarted and botched several high-profile murder cases along the line until their imprisonment; the last matter resulting in failure to identify serial killer Rex Heuerman, whom law enforcement could have apprehended thirteen years earlier in time! This last unfolding leads up to the courageous and competent formation of the Gilgo Beach Homicide Investigation Task Force, set in place by Suffolk County Police Commissioner Rodney Harrison, including cooperating inter-agencies from local, state, and federal governments: Suffolk County District Attorney Ray Tierney's office, Suffolk County Sheriff Errol Toulon, Jr.'s office, New York State Police, and the FBI.

CAST Of NONFICTIONAL CHARACTERS

Bellone, Steve ~ County executive, Suffolk County.

Bissett, Jimmy ~ Wealthy businessman and co-owner of the Long Island Aquarium and Exhibition Center, including the Hyatt Place Hotel in Riverhead ~ supposedly committed suicide ~ purportedly connected to the LISK case on several levels.

Bittrolff, John ~ Known as the Manorville Butcher. Convicted murderer and suspect in the Long Island Serial Killer case.

Bombace, Detective Kenneth ~ One of several cops involved in the former Chief of Police James Burke cover-up, including participation in the Christopher Loeb beating.

Brennan, Barbara ~ Oak Beach resident, one of whose door Shannan Gilbert knocked on the morning of her disappearance.

Brensic, Robert ~ One of four youths found guilty in the 1979 murder trial of 13-year-old-Johnny Pius; later acquitted.

Brewer, Joseph ~ Owner of the home at 8 The Fairway, Oak Beach, from which Shannan Gilbert fled, screaming for her life.

Burke, James C. ~ Disgraced and convicted former chief of the Suffolk County Police Department.

Coletti, Gus ~ Oak Beach resident who tried to help Shannan Gilbert by calling 911 on the morning of her disappearance.

Cottingham, Detective Thomas ~ Suffolk County Police Department. One of several cops involved in the James Burke cover-up.

Cuff, Patrick ~ Suffolk County police commander whom James Burke, after being made chief of police, went after with a vengeance and retaliation referencing an internal affairs investigation into Burke and known prostitute Lowrita Rickenbacker.

Draiss, Officer Brian ~ Suffolk County Police Department. One of several cops involved in the James Burke cover-up.

Gilbert, Shannan ~ Craigslist sex worker victim whose remains led to the discovery of the 'Gilgo Four.'

Gilgo Four: Maureen Brainard-Barnes, Megan Waterman, Melissa Barthelemy, Amber Lynn Costello.

Hackett, Peter C. ~ Former police surgeon for Suffolk County's Emergency Services, neighbor of Joseph Brewer, Oak Beach.

Harrison, Rodney ~ Newly appointed Suffolk County Police Commissioner, 2022. Created the Suffolk County Gilgo Beach Homicide Investigation Task Force.

Hart, Geraldine ~ Former FBI Agent; former police commissioner, Suffolk County; presently, Director of Public Safety, Hofstra University, Hempstead, New York.

Heuermann, Rex Andrew, age 60 ~ Arrested and charged with the murders of Megan Waterman, Amber Lynn Costello, Melissa Barthelemy. Prime suspect in the murder of Maureen Brainard-Barnes.

Heuermann, Asa Ellerup-Heuermann, age 60 ~ wife of Rex Heuermann [children: Christopher Sheridan, age 33 (by Ellerup's previous marriage) & Victoria Heuermann, age 26].

Hickey, James ~ Former Suffolk County police lieutenant and star witness for the prosecution who testified against former district attorney Thomas Spota and the former head of the Anti-Corruption

Bureau, Christopher McPartland in the trial of convicted former chief of police James Burke.

Kelly, Sergeant Michael ~ Suffolk County Police Department. One of several cops involved in the James Burke cover-up.

Lanieri, Robert ~ Food services executive for the Long Island Aquarium, who committed suicide ~ see Bissett, Jimmy.

Lenart, Tiffany ~ Digital Forensics Expert ~ Cyber Crime Detective.

Leto, Detective Anthony ~ Suffolk County Police Department. One of several cops involved in the former Chief of Police James Burke cover-up, including participation in the Christopher Loeb beating.

Macedonio, Robert ~ attorney for Asa Ellerup (Rex Heuermann's wife).

Malone, Guy ~ Insurance fraud investigator whose wife was purportedly working as a 'sporting girl,' protected by, and part and parcel to, then police sergeant James Burke's prostitution network.

Malone, Heather ~ Whose husband (Guy Malone) brought to light the nefarious dealings of then police officer James Burke.

McPartland, Christopher ~ Disgraced and convicted former chief prosecutor of the Anti-Corruption Bureau for the district attorney's office, Suffolk County.

Mitev, Vess ~ attorney for Asa Ellerup-Heuermann's two adult children.

Nealis, Detective Christopher ~ Suffolk County Police Department. One of many cops involved in the James Burke cover-up.

Pak, Michael ~ Shannan Gilbert's driver/bodyguard on May 1, 2010.

Quartararo, Michael ~ One of four youths found guilty in the 1979 murder trial of 13-year-old Johnny Pius; later acquitted.

Quartararo, Peter ~ One of four youths found guilty in the 1979 murder trial of 13-year-old Johnny Pius; later acquitted.

Ray, John ~ Attorney for the Gilbert estate: Mari Gilbert (mother); Sarra, Sherre, Stevie, Shannan (daughters).

Regensburg, Detective Kenneth ~ Suffolk County Police Department. One of many cops involved in the James Burke cover-up.

Rickenbacker, Lowrita ~ Known prostitute with whom then Sergeant James Burke, Suffolk County, was sexually involved.

Ruggiero, Francine ~ Christopher Loeb's probation officer.

Ryan, Thomas ~ One of four youths found guilty in the 1979 murder trial of 13-year-old Johnny Pius; later acquitted.

Schaller, Dave ~ Friend/roommate of Amber Lynn Costello ~ Gilgo Beach murder victim.

Sinclair, Detective Keith ~ Suffolk County Police Department. One of many cops involved in the James Burke cover-up.

Spota, Thomas ~ Disgraced and convicted former district attorney, Suffolk County.

Stephan, Vincent ~ Detective, Suffolk County Police Department.

Tierney, Ray ~ Newly elected Suffolk County District Attorney, 2022.

Toulon, Errol D., Jr. ~ Suffolk County Sheriff.

Varrone, Dominick ~ Former chief of detectives, Suffolk County, re Gilgo Beach serial killer case ~ removed from case by former chief of police James Burke.

Note: "Leanne" [actual name withheld] ~ woman identified as "Leanne" ~ affidavit stating that she had paid sexual relations with then Inspector James Burke of the Organized Crime Bureau, Suffolk County, at a cocaine-fueled house party in Oak Beach ~ John Ray (attorney) represents Leanne. Ray also represents the Shannan Gilbert and Jessica Taylor families.

Maureen Brainard-Barnes, 25 years old, 4 feet 11 inches tall, disappeared 2007. Remains found December 14, 2010.

Melissa Barthelemy, 24 years old, 4 feet 10 inches tall, disappeared 2009. First victim found on December 11, 2010.

Megan Waterman, 22 years old, 5 feet 5 inches tall, disappeared June 2010. Body was found December 13, 2010.

Amber Lynn Costello, 27 years old, 5 feet tall, disappeared September 2010. Remains found December 13, 2010.

BOOK ONE

CHAPTER ONE

On Saturday May 1, 2010, Shannan Gilbert, a sex worker, ran from a client's home in Oak Beach, Long Island, New York, screaming for her life. Suddenly, she had vanished. Nineteen months had elapsed before her body was discovered by Suffolk County Police in December of 2011. Ironically, it was while searching for Shannan in Oak Beach that eventually led police to discover four victims in nearby Gilgo Beach: Melissa Barthelemy, Megan Waterman, Amber Lynn Costello, and Maureen Brainard-Barnes. They have been dubbed the Gilgo Four. All sex workers. The four bodies were discovered by police searching the thick, scraggly stretch of underbrush along Ocean Parkway, Long Island, New York. This discovery was followed shortly by an additional six bodies, including an Asian male and a female toddler for a total of ten victims found in the Gilgo Beach area. The toddler is believed to be 2 to 3 years of age, found with gold jewelry; earrings and necklace. The child was later identified as belonging to the mother of an unidentified victim referred to as "Peaches," Jane Doe #3, because of a tattoo located on her left breast. She was found 7 miles away from her child. Shannan Gilbert was found in December 2011 at Oak Beach.

A suspect, 60-year-old architect, husband, and father of two, Rex Andrew Heuermann, residing in Massapequa Park, was arrested near his Manhattan firm on the evening of Thursday July 13, 2023. He has been charged with first- and second-degree murder referencing three of the victims: Melissa Barthelemy, Megan Waterman, Amber Lynn Costello. He is also the prime suspect in the murder of the fourth sex worker, Maureen Brainard-Barnes, whose body was also found close by. Gilgo Beach is approximately 15 miles from the Heuermann's Massapequa Park home. Law enforcement was seen entering the Manhattan firm at 385 Fifth Avenue with crowbars and sledgehammers in hand. At the same time, his home in Massapequa Park was being raided by police. The evidence linking Heuermann to the trio is overwhelming.

Heuermann was later taken to police headquarters in Yaphank, from there to Riverhead Correctional Facility (jail), where he is currently confined until trial. He has since been taken off suicide watch and placed in a 60-square-foot cell. He reads, watches television, goes for walks alone in a small recreation area, and sees a clergyman once a week.

As part of the ongoing investigation, two prostitutes were interviewed by police in late July who were hired by Heuermann and said they feared for their safety during their encounters, having accused him of being "violent" and "aggressive" towards them.

To this day, authorities do not believe that Shannan Gilbert was the victim of foul play but rather the victim of a so-called "misadventure." She was found a quarter mile from a client's home, Joseph Brewer, in a marshy area. Police say she likely became disoriented and drowned. Skeptics disputed that claim, particularly Shannan's family and their estate attorney John Ray. Also, renowned independent medical examiner Michael Baden (former medical examiner for New York City), noted that Shannan's hyoid bone had been fractured. Baden pointed out that a fractured or broken hyoid bone is typical of someone who has been strangled. However, after a period of nineteen months, while being subject to the elements, deterioration of that bone may have been the result of animal infestation.

With the advancement of forensic science, coupled to what law enforcement can now achieve referencing burner phones and cellular data, there are very few crimes that can go unsolved today. But it takes the collective cooperation among local police departments working alongside state and federal agencies to make this fly. That is what we saw with the newly created Gilgo Beach Homicide Investigation Task Force in February 2021 coming together as a whole. The team was assembled by Suffolk County Police Commissioner Rodney K. Harrison in conjunction with newly elected District Attorney Ray Tierney, and other law enforcement agencies.

Rex Andrew Heuermann utilized burner phones and e-mail aliases to thwart detection—or so he thought. Burner phones *are indeed* traceable as one must establish an e-mail or some sort of identifiable information. Cellular data in conjunction with location data was utilized to pinpoint the potential suspect in a particular proximity. Genetic genealogy initially played a major role, which eventually led to one victim's identification, and then another. DNA analysis of an "abandonment sample" of pizza crust along with a napkin obtained by a federal agent from the trash outside Heuermann's Midtown Manhattan office helped put a significant nail in the man's coffin.

Mitochondrial DNA was used as evidence for the first time in US courts in 1998, and it has since become a staple in many cases where DNA evidence is presented. Law enforcement agencies working closely together on local, state, and federal levels are needed to solve many cold case files. Once again, these cases are, indeed, solvable.

As the story unfolded, we learned that Rex Heuermann owns property in South Carolina and a time-share in Las Vegas, Nevada. While under police surveillance for several months as the task team built their case against Rex Heuermann, the suspect continued to use the services of sex workers. There came a point when the Gilgo Beach Homicide Investigation Task Force team believed that Heuermann might attempt to flee the country or strike again, and so authorities arrested him at that juncture as the situation was growing dangerous.

For over a decade, the initial Gilgo Beach murder investigation under Suffolk County Police Chief James Burke, District Attorney Thomas Spota, and Anti-corruption Bureau Chief Christopher McPartland failed to solve the Gilgo Beach murders. The reasons are varied. For openers, Chief of Police James Burke did not want attention focused on the area that was his playground; that is, the Gilgo Beach/Oak Beach arena. Why? Because it was where he and his cronies 'partied,' partaking in cocaine-fueled sex parties. Also, Burke was being looked at by the FBI for the severe beating of a prisoner in police custody. Too, as a general rule, the police did not take the disappearance of sex workers very seriously. An important lead that pointed to a suspect in the Long Island serial murders was disregarded. Quite frankly, the administration bungled the case. More accurately, the then Chief of Police James Burke thwarted the investigation at every turn. He, in fact, kept the FBI from investigating those murders by utilizing "initial jurisdiction" gibberish and "duplicative work" rubbish, successfully keeping the Feds at arm's length.

As early as 2010, the police investigation referencing the Gilgo Beach murders, conducted under then Suffolk County Chief of Police James Burke, District Attorney Thomas Spota, and Anti-corruption Bureau Chief Christopher McPartland had received a very good tip from Amber Costello's pimp regarding a suspect: the man's distinguishing features, including the make and model of the vehicle he drove. Yet the police neglected to thoroughly investigate the matter; that is, until the newly formed Gilgo Beach Homicide Investigation Task Force was brought into play under Police Commissioner Rodney Harrison and District Attorney Ray Tierney.

To *fully* understand the reasoning behind the reluctance to properly investigate matters of such magnitude, one would have to comprehend the "Culture of Corruption" concerning Suffolk County law enforcement dating back as early as 1979—beginning with the Johnny Pius murder case.

Two key players, with whom you are familiar, raise their ugly heads. A very young Jimmy Burke and an aspiring prosecutor, Thomas Spota. Jimmy was Spota's star witness in the Johnny Pius murder case. Jimmy's testimony helped seal the fate of the four teenage defendants charged with the crime. Here is their decades-long story, and others, told in brief.

CHAPTER TWO

A CULTURE OF CORRUPTION CONCERNING SUFFOLK COUNTY LAW ENFORCEMENT ~ 1979–2021

CRONYISM, COLLUSION, CONSPIRACY, COERCED CONFESSIONS & COVER-UPS

Former Chief of Police James Burke was arrested and sentenced to 46 months for the beating of a handcuffed/shackled prisoner, Christopher Loeb, while in police custody at the Fourth Precinct police headquarters in Smithtown in 2012.

A culture of corruption referencing Suffolk County's law enforcement agencies did not begin with the incarceration of James Burke back in December of 2015. Hopefully, it ended with the imprisonment of Thomas Spota, its former district attorney, along with his former Anti-corruption Bureau Chief Christopher McPartland, on December 10, 2021. Three bad apples that contaminated the barrel.

Former Suffolk County Police Chief James Burke

Left: Former Suffolk County District Attorney Thomas Spota
Right: Former Suffolk County Anti-Corruption Bureau Chief Christopher McPartland

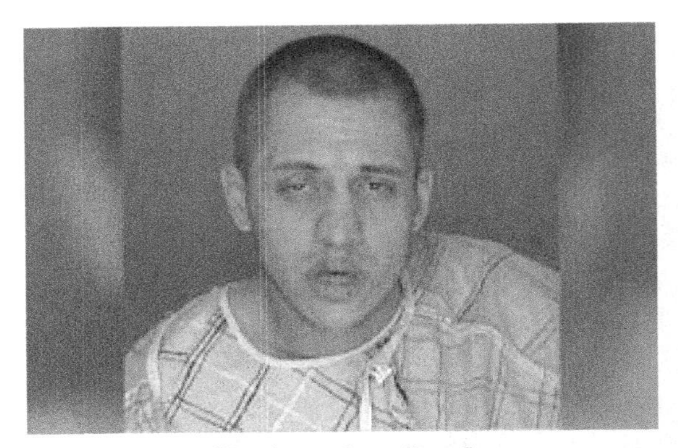

Christopher Loeb

Thomas Spota and Christopher McPartland each received 5-year prison terms for the cover-up assault and violation of Christopher Loeb's civil rights, inclusive of obstruction of justice, witness tampering, and conspiracy—all directly relating to the police chief's severe beating of Loeb. Additionally, Spota received a fine of $100,000.

A culture of corruption can be documented decades ago in the words, writings, and wisdom of retired Suffolk County Court Judge Stuart Namm. Judge Stuart Namm spent sixteen plus years on the bench before writing a book titled *A Whistleblower's Lament: The Perverted Pursuit of Justice in the State of New York*. It is a courageous testament.

Retired Judge Stuart Namm

Judge Stuart Namm's memoirs addressed many cases through those years. One case in particular is the Johnny Pius case, which Namm described as "A Microcosm of Middle America." In other words, the culturally rural and suburban areas of the United States. Peter Quartararo and his younger brother, Michael Quartararo, received life sentences for the 1979 murder of 13-year-old Johnny Pius. It was now late 1985, and there was unfinished business to attend to: the retrial and trial of the two older boys, Robert Brensic and Thomas Ryan. They were scheduled on the judge's calendar, the presiding judge of the Suffolk County Court, Judge Stuart Namm. Namm was monikered "The Hanging Judge," "The Frank Serpico of Judges," and "Maximum Stu."

Johnny Pius

Thomas Ryan

The jury, in two separate trials, found the evidence in both cases sufficient: guilty. Judge Namm sentenced Robert Brensic and Thomas Ryan to the max: 25-years to-life. A decade later, three of the four convictions had been reversed by state and federal courts. Peter and Michael Quartararo had each served approximately nine years in prison (Michael having been made part of a work release program). Robert Brensic had served almost ten years. Thomas Ryan, initially refusing to take any plea deal, spent almost eighteen years in prison maintaining his innocence before finally caving. He had to say he was guilty under oath.

Ultimately, it took Judge Stuart Namm a good many years on the bench before noting an emerging pattern, realizing that he was being used, mislead, outright lied to, and that corruption was prevalent in Suffolk County's homicide squad, the district attorney's office, the forensic laboratory — and that innocent people do go to prison while the guilty go unpunished.

Names in other criminal cases such as Jerry Steuerman and his son Todd Steuerman kept cropping up as those who escaped justice, along with names like Joseph Creedon, Peter Kent, and Glenn Harris. Two high-profile cases that highlight and underscore travesties of justice personified are the Johnny Pius and Marty Tankleff cases. You might be asking yourself: What do those cases have to do with Jimmy Burke, Thomas Spota, and others like Christopher McPartland? The short answer is that to fully understand how this corruption first began, developed, and spread like a cancer, it is necessary to go back to the very beginning, 1979, and view the relationship between Thomas Spota and young Jimmy Burke, noting along the way how that duo formed a bond, shaped and perpetuated a culture of corruption—eventually erecting a criminal empire in Suffolk County.

Jerry Steuerman

Marty Tankleff

Johnny Pius was murdered on April 20, 1979. The police had rounded up the four teenage boys and taken them to homicide squad headquarters. Initially, the police denied that they were holding the four youths until later that evening a parent had spotted a car belonging to one of the boys parked at headquarters.

In the interrogation room, detectives elicited a *false confession* from Peter Quartararo, then drove the 15-year-old to the crime scene area to feed him details to support that *bogus confessio*n. Detectives Anthony Palumbo and Gary Leonard were at the forefront of the investigation. Michael Quartararo was 14 years old at the time of the murder, Peter Quartararo 15, Robert Brensic 17, Thomas Ryan 17. Peter had given the detectives what they wanted to hear: a false confession. There were glaring inconsistencies in Peter's supposed *confession.*

The Pius murder case was the biggest case of prosecutor Thomas Spota's career at that point in time. But Spota needed a witness in addition to Peter Quartararo's *confession*. Spota had 18-year-old James Burke as his star witness.

A recap: The first trial began two years later in May of 1981. Peter and Michael Quartararo were tried together. Peter spent nine years in prison, never retried after the first conviction. Michael Quartararo was sentenced to nine years, part of which became a work release program. Robert Brensic spent 10 years in prison. Thomas Ryan spent almost 18 years in prison. There had been several subsequent trials. Thomas was the last defendant to be tried. He was reconvicted in a second trial. A third ended in a mistrial. It would have been the eighth trial referencing the four boys. All four verdicts were later overturned on appeal by state and federal courts. The arrest and incarceration of these four teenagers charged with the murder of thirteen-year-old Johnny Pius of Smithtown is a remarkable tale. However, no less remarkable than the tale of Marty Tankleff.

Marty Tankleff Story: Martin Tankleff Murder Case: September 7, 1988.

A noted journalist, Richard Firstman, along with a prominent NYPD detective (retired), Jay Salpeter, turned private investigator, eventually helped free an innocent man from prison by respectively reporting and reinvestigating a sensational murder case involving a then 17-year-old boy accused of killing his adoptive parents—for which he spent 17-plus-years in prison_for those crimes that he did not commit. The tale is extraordinary, told by Firstman and Salpeter in their book titled *A Criminal Injustice*. It is the Marty Tankleff story. The men involved in those murders were never prosecuted.

What is remarkable is that several of the same names of those law enforcement officials suspected of and/or charged with perverting the course of justice kept cropping up over the course of many years—murder case after murder case. Unscrupulous men who put innocent people behind bars and/or allowed culpable criminals to evade justice. One such name was K. James McCready of the Suffolk County homicide squad. I'll cover McCready's duplicitous behavior shortly, for he is the poster boy for bad cops to follow in the eighties as he paves the way for the likes of Jimmy Burke to follow suit.

A recently published book that primarily deals with James Burke is titled *Jimmy the King*: *Murder, Vice, and the Reign of a Dirty Cop*, authored by Gus Garcia-Roberts, investigative reporter for such news outlets as *The Washington Post*, *Los Angeles Times, USA Today,* and *Newsday.* The nonfiction books mentioned here very much cover a culture of corruption as it pertains to Suffolk County, Long Island, New York, especially with the aforesaid murder cases.

Along the lines of police misconduct, I dealt with other less sensational criminal cases back in Bayside, Queens, one of which involved an innocent young man who went to prison for a crime he did not commit. I contributed to helping in his release by writing nine editorials (eight were extensive) for a local paper (*The Towers News*). I was working indirectly with noted Manhattan criminal defense attorney Barry Slotnick, his partner Mark Baker, and Mike Taibbi of CBS News at the time. Richard Tchilinguirian was railroaded by the Queens police for the attempted rape of a high-ranking police officer's daughter.

Two no-nos to steer clear of concerning a criminal matter:

1. Withholding exculpatory evidence; that is, any evidence tending to exonerate a person of guilt.

2. Suborning perjury: inducing a person to give false information, especially under oath.

The police committed both of the above offenses re the Richard Tchilinguirian matter. Richard received a sentence of 18 to 54 months. New evidence surfaced, but Richard had already served 16 months before the verdict was finally overturned. A bittersweet moment for family and friends.

To date, I've written eleven murder/mystery novels. Several are based on or inspired by true crime stories, the latter two of which were published under the umbrella of New Journalism; that is, a combining of fact and fiction involving the **LISK** (**L**ong **I**sland **S**erial **K**iller) murders. The first book is appropriately titled ***The Long Island Serial Killer Murders ~ Gilgo Beach and Beyond.*** The second is its sequel, ***Snuff Stuff.*** The fictional/nonfictional treatment of these last two works allowed me to suppose this and surmise that. In *Snuff Stuff*, a cast of fictional and nonfictional characters are listed in alphabetical order and designated with an asterisk for easy reference. Actual names will jump off these pages as the story unfolds, certainly recognizable to those familiar with these murderous events.

In this purely nonfictional accounting of a perhaps multi-regional serial killer titled *The Long-Awaited Arrest of Long Island Serial Killer Rex Heuermann ~ Past "Administration" to Blame*, Heuermann may prove to be the ultimate bogeyman. Ironically, a Culture of Corruption concerning Suffolk County law enforcement—incorporating Cronyism, Collusion, Conspiracy, Coerced Confessions, and Cover-Ups—eventually led to this inexcusable conclusion. Within these pages is pure fact. No fiction whatsoever, except where I expressly point out conjecture. This chronical is comprised of sheer, unadulterated events, unabashedly presented to reveal the absolute truth of this perpetual deplorable decades-old situation; that is, up until the period nearing the formation of the Gilgo Beach Homicide Investigation Task Force.

The information I impart here, reveals corruption throughout the country, not just a particular county. However, the matter was never more prevalent than a *Culture of Corruption* persisting in Suffolk County law enforcement, boasting a murder conviction rate, based on suspects' supposed *confessions*, of 95–97 percent. It is an unprecedented number throughout the rest of the country. So brazen was the Suffolk County homicide squad's braggadocio, that they boldly garbed themselves in T-shirts displaying that percentage rate at various police functions; 95–97%.

This A+ performance rating was primarily the result of *false, coerced confessions*. Period. Trickery (legal that is) is fair game within the walls of the interrogation room (euphemistically referred to as the *interview* room); coercion and police brutality are not permitted. Yet, a plethora of violent reports across the years, exhibiting such tactics by police, was the norm rather than the exception. For example, an interrogator placing a thick phone directory upon a suspect's head then slamming the book with a policeman's billy club (blackjack) is but one such tactic. Employing the same method upon a victim's chest, shoulders, arms, and legs leaves no bruises. Sleep and food deprivation are other forms of punishment. What homicide detectives do *feed* their suspects in a good many situations are the words the police wish their prisoners to recite, then sign off on; in other words, a rehearsed false confession as to what the detectives *believed* happened, and with very little investigation to support their convictions. Such was the situation referencing the Johnny Pius murder case, along with many others.

To unfold a detailed account of each case would fill an encyclopedia, not simply a single book. Too, you would be muddled in minutiae. So, rather than head in that direction, I will highlight the corruption that went on for decades involving the police, homicide, the anti-corruption bureau, and the district attorney's office, illustrating why several of these law enforcement officials, who were supposedly there to serve and protect, did what they did. The reasons as to behavior are generally twofold: greed and penultimate power.

The Johnny Pius Murder Case: April 1979

Martin Tankleff Murder Case: September 7, 1988

Richard Tchilinguirian story: arrested September 1989 for the attempted rape of a high-ranking police officer's daughter. I started reporting the story in March of 1991 via several editorials. Richard was released from prison December 1991. He died shortly thereafter from cancer.

CHAPTER THREE

Shannan Gilbert, a sex worker, went missing in the early morning hours of May 1, 2010 from her client's home, Joseph Brewer, in Oak Beach, screaming for her life: "They're trying to kill me," she said to a 911 operator. Oak Beach is a town of Babylon, Suffolk County, literally just a few minutes drive away from Gilgo Beach.

Shannan Gilbert

Joseph Brewer

May 13, 2022

Detective Lieutenant Kevin Beyrer, Office of the Suffolk County Police Homicide Section:

Detective Lieutenant Kevin Beyrer

"This video is made to explain the circumstances surrounding the three 911 calls made on the day Shannan Gilbert went missing," says Beyrer. "The full non-edited 911 calls are available, and I encourage people to listen to them in their entirety. Portions of the call taken out of context would sound sensational.

"During the early morning hours of May 1, 2010, Shannan Gilbert, a Craigslist sex worker and resident of Jersey City, New Jersey, traveled from Manhattan to meet a client, Joseph Brewer, at his home at 8 The Fairway, Oak Beach, New York. Shannan was driven to Oak Beach from Manhattan by her driver, Michael Pak. Neither of them was familiar with the area, none of them had been there before, neither of them had met Brewer before. Pak waited in the car while Shannan was inside with Brewer. Pak was her de facto security.

"At 4:51 a.m., while at Brewer's house, Shannan called 911. This call lasted for more than 21 minutes. At times, Shannan is speaking calmly, but slurring her words. At times, she's not responsive, and at times she is screaming. During this call, Brewer and

Pak are heard trying to get Shannan to leave the house. Shannan eventually does leave the house and runs to Gus Coletti's house, located at 17 The Fairway, which causes him to call 911 at 5:22 a.m."

OAK BEACH, NEW YORK. FULL 911 CALL:

NYS 911 Operator: State Police Trooper Frye. State Police.

Shannan Gilbert: Yeah, there's somebody after me.

NYS 911 Operator: I'm sorry?

Shannan Gilbert: There's somebody after me.

NYS 911 Operator: Where are you?

Shannan Gilbert: There's somebody after me.

NYS 911 Operator: Ok, where are you?

Shannan Gilbert: There's somebody after me.

NYS 911 Operator: Where are you, ma'am?

Shannan Gilbert: I don't know.

NYS 911 Operator: Are you driving right now?

Shannan Gilbert: No, I'm inside the house.

NYS 911 Operator: I'm sorry?

Shannan Gilbert: I'm inside a house.

NYS 911 Operator: What house?

Shannan Gilbert: I don't know. Can you trace where I am?

NYS 911 Operator: I'm sorry?

Shannan Gilbert: Can you trace where I am?

NYS 911 Operator: No, I can't. What's your call back number you are calling from?

Shannan Gilbert: Huh?

NYS 911 Operator: What number are you calling from?

Shannan Gilbert: Somebody's after me. Please.

NYS 911 Operator: Are you in Nassau County or Suffolk County?

Shannan Gilbert: Um, I'm in Long Island.

NYS 911 Operator: Where on Long Island are you?

Joseph Brewer: Yeah, he wants to talk to you, the guy wants to talk to you.

Shannan Gilbert: No

Joseph Brewer: Go ahead, talk to her.

Shannan Gilbert: No.

Joseph Brewer: *INAUDIBLE*

Shannan Gilbert: No. No. Stop no.

Joseph Brewer: *INAUDIBLE*

NYS 911 Operator: Where in Long Island are you? Suffolk County? Nassau County?

Shannan Gilbert: Huh?

Joseph Brewer: *INAUDIBLE*

Shannan Gilbert: Alright.

Michael Pak: *INAUDIBLE*

Shannan Gilbert: Why are you calling me by my name?

Michael Pak: *INAUDIBLE*

Shannan Gilbert: Why?

NYS 911 Operator: What county are you on the line?

Shannan Gilbert: Stop.

Joseph Brewer: *INAUDIBLE*

Shannan Gilbert: Stop it, please.

Michael Pak: You ok?

Shannan Gilbert: Please stop.

Joseph Brewer: Alright. *INAUDIBLE*

Shannan Gilbert: Please can you shut the door?

Joseph Brewer: No, time to go.

Shannan Gilbert: Please.

Michael Pak: You ok?

Shannan Gilbert: Please.

Joseph Brewer: *INAUDIBLE*

Shannan Gilbert: Please.

Joseph Brewer: *INAUDIBLE* Come on, let's go. We'll all go outside. Come on, going outside, all of us. Come on, all of us, come on, we're all going outside. Come on.

Shannan Gilbert: No, please.

Joseph Brewer: *INAUDIBLE* Come on, please, come on.

Shannon Gilbert: Please.

Joseph Brewer: Please, come on.

Shannan Gilbert: Why?

Joseph Brewer: Please come out here.

Brewer and Pak continue to try and convince Shannan to leave the premises.

Joseph Brewer: I'll go upstairs, I'll go upstairs, you leave. Hey, look, I'm going upstairs, you leave. I'm going upstairs, you leave. Ok? You leave please.

Joseph Brewer: Take care.

Michael Pak: Take care.

INAUDIBLE

Michael Pak: Whoa, whoa. What's the matter? Are you ok?

Shannan Gilbert: What are you going to do?

Michael Pak: *INAUDIBLE*

Shannan Gilbert: What are you going to do to me?

Michael Pak: *INAUDIBLE*

Shannan Gilbert: Why?

NYS 911 Operator: Huh, I don't know *INAUDIBLE*

Shannan Gilbert: Why? *INAUDIBLE* You going to kill me?

Michael Pak: Are you crazy?

NYS 911 Operator: *INAUDIBLE* It's trying to, I think it's trying to *INAUDIBLE*

Michael Pak: No

Shannan Gilbert: Why are you going to kill me?

NYS 911 Operator: *INAUDIBLE*

Michael Pak: Come on, you're freaking me out. Come on let's go.

Shannan Gilbert: Out in the middle of nowhere?

Michael Pak: Let's go back, let's go back to Manhattan, alright? We're in Long Island, near the water so, the ocean.

Shannan Gilbert: Please stop.

Michael Pak: Come on, it's me, Mike. Come on let's go.

Shannan Gilbert: No. Stop it, please.

A second 911 NYS Operator joins the call.

NYS 911 Operator: Hello?

Michael Pak: *INAUDIBLE*

NYS 911 Operator: Hello?

Shannan Gilbert: Please.

NYS 911 Operator: What's, what's, what's the problem, what's the matter? What happened?

NYS 911 Operator: Hello?

Shannan Gilbert: Please get me out of here Mike.

Michael Pak: *INAUDIBLE*

NYS 911 Operator: Hello?

Shannan Gilbert: You're being sarcastic.

Michael Pak: About what?

Shannan Gilbert: About this…You are a part of this all along.

Michael Pak: I just met him just now…*INAUDIBLE*

Lt. Beyrer Narration: “Shannon then ran from Brewer’s at 8 The Fairway to Gus Coletti’s house at 17 The Fairway, a distance of two-tenths of a mile.”

Background Noise:

NYS 911 Operator: Shannan.

Background Noise:

Shannan Gilbert: “Screaming.”

Background Noise:

Lt. Beyrer Narration: “Shannan interacts with Coletti. He invites her inside his home.”

Shannan knocks on Coletti’s door.

NYS 911 Operator: Shannan.

Gus Coletti: What’s the matter? Is somebody after you? Huh?

NYS 911 Operator: Hello. Hello.

Shannan Gilbert: *INAUDIBLE*

Gus Coletti: Are you alright?

Shannan Gilbert: I need help.

Gus Coletti: Don’t get yourself hurt. Where are you going?

Shannan Gilbert: “Heavy breathing.”

Gus Coletti: Where are you going? What are you doing?

Lt. Beyrer Narration: “She then runs from Coletti’s home, prompting Coletti to call 911. This is where Shannan’s call ends. After Coletti’s call, Shannan then runs another two-tenths of a mile to another home at 43 The Bayou, prompting a third 911 call made at 5:30 a.m. by Barbara Brennan."

SCPD 911 Operator: Suffolk Police what's the location of your emergency?

Gus Coletti: Yes, this, I live in Oak Beach in the Association. There's a young girl about 14 years old running around here screaming, and there's some guy trying to follow her.

SCPD 911 Operator: What's the address there?

Gus Coletti: I'm at 17 The Fairway.

SCPD 911 Operator: Alright. You have a description of the girl or the boy?

Gus Coletti: Pardon me?

SCPD 911 Operator: Alright. You have a description of the girl or the boy?

Gus Coletti: The girl is about 14 years old, blonde hair, very small. The boy I can't tell; he was in like uh…a suburban.

SCPD 911 Operator: What color?

Gus Coletti: Uh, black?

Michael Pak, Shannan's driver, was operating a black SUV.

SCPD 911 Operator: Did you happen to get a plate number or anything?

Gus Coletti: No, I didn't.

SCPD 911 Operator: Ok, telephone number you're calling from?

Gus Coletti: --- ----

SCPD 911 Operator: Are they still on The Fairway?

Gus Coletti: Uh, they just went past the gatehouse where the entrance is.

SCPD 911 Operator: And what's the name of the complex?

Gus Coletti: It's Oak Beach Association.

SCPD 911 Operator: Ok.

Gus Coletti: Out at, by Robert Moses.

SCPD 911 Operator: Alright, we'll get somebody over there.

Gus Coletti: I'll be watching.

SCPD 911 Operator: Oh, ok.

Gus Coletti: Bye.

Shannan Gilbert then knocks on Barbara Brennan's door, prompting a third 911 call.

SCPD 911 Operator: Suffolk police 875, what is the location of your emergency?

Barbara Brennan: 40…43 The Bayou. Some woman is knocking at my door.

SCPD 911 Operator: What town are you in?

Barbara Brennan: Oak Beach Association.

SCPD 911 Operator: What's the nearest corner street, ma'am?

Barbara Brennan: Ocean Parkway. She says she's in danger.

SCPD 911 Operator: Do you know her, or not?

Barbara Brennan: No, I don't. I'm not letting her in.

SCPD 911 Operator: She banging on your door now?

Barbara Brennan: Yeah.

SCPD 911 Operator: Did she say what kind of danger?

Barbara Brennan: No.

SCPD 911 Operator: Oh.

Barbara Brennan: And we live in a gated community.

SCPD 911 Operator: What's your name, ma'am?

Barbara Brennan : Barbara Brennan.

SCPD 911 Operator: Is there a name to that community?

Barbara Brennan: Uh, Oak Beach Association.

SCPD 911 Operator: Oak Beach Association.

Barbara Brennan: And I have an elderly mother here.

SCPD 911 Operator: Alright, I'll get somebody right over there, ok?

Barbara Brennan: Ok. Thank you.

SCPD 911 Operator: You're welcome.

Lt. Kevin Beyrer Narration: "This (the video) shows drone footage shot from the ground showing the marshland. It was taken at the same time of the year and time of day as when Shannan went missing. These reeds can grow over 12 feet tall. They can disorient someone inside them, causing them to lose a sense of direction. One cannot tell where the highway is or the bay is. The reeds and brush can become impenetrable in places. There's a trench running east and west through the marshland. This was created to allow mosquito control. It is believed that Shannan followed this trench. Personal belongings of hers were found just north of the trench. Shannan's remains were found north of the trench about 158 feet south of Ocean Parkway, approximately three quarters of a mile from where she was last seen.

There's been information received during the course of this investigation that other people may be involved in this incident. They have all been investigated, and there is no reason at this time to believe that anyone else is involved in this tragic series of events.

"The police responded to Coletti's and Brennan's 911 calls. Pak, Brewer and Shannan were all gone. Gus Coletti provided a description of Pak's car, which was also gone. This created the possibility that Shannan had been driven out of the area, which caused delay in the initial search for her. The police department has thoroughly investigated this case for more than a decade. The official cause of Shannan's death is undetermined. This official classification means that there is insufficient or no evidence to determine or even to exclude a cause of death. The Gilbert family hired a private pathologist to conduct an autopsy. His determination is there is insufficient information to determine a definite cause of death, but the autopsy's findings are consistent with homicidal strangulation. That pathologist report will be made available.

"This case, including the 911 call and all of the other cases commonly referred to as Gilgo, in their entirety, were made available to the Behavioral Analysis Unit or BAU of the FBI. As part of BAU's review of the case, they retained the services of a psychiatrist to review Shannan's words and actions on the 911 tape, and also to review the facts of the case. BAU's opinion, based on their review of Shannan's case, the scene, the 911 calls, and the psychiatrist's review, is that Shannan Gilbert's death is not consistent with Shannan being the victim or violence or a violent offender. Significant differences between Shannan's death and the circumstances surrounding the other victims' deaths were also highlighted by the BAU.

"The Suffolk County Police Department is open to evaluate any evidence to be able to help us and all involved to determine an actual cause of death. However, based on the evidence, the facts, and the totality of the circumstances, the prevailing opinion is that

Shannan's death, while tragic, was not a murder and most likely an accident."

Over the course of a nineteen-month period while searching for Shannan Gilbert in Oak Beach, police discover the bodies of several victims in a wooded area in nearby Gilgo Beach. The first set of remains were referred to as the Gilgo Four: Maureen Brainard-Barnes, Amber Lynn Costello, Megan Waterman, Melissa Barthelemy. In December of 2011, Shannan's body was found in a marsh in the back of Peter Hackett's Oak Beach home. Hackett was never considered a possible suspect, nor were Joseph Brewer or Shannan's escort driver/pimp, Michael Pak.

Left to Right: Maureen Brainard-Barnes, Amber Lynn Costello, Megan Waterman, Melissa Barthelemy

Dr. Peter Hackett

CHAPTER FOUR

James Burke: The Early Years

To get a sense of just how bad James Conway Burke was from an early age, we must to go back to his childhood days. By age 12, Jimmy had been engaged in nefarious dealings. Jimmy, a juvenile delinquent, was busy breaking into homes, stealing jewelry, especially gold jewelry. He knew precisely what pawnshops would deal in questionably obtained jewelry. Also, Jimmy was selling marijuana to his schoolmates, and occasionally dealing in heroin. By age 18, he would become attorney Thomas Spota's star witness in the sensational murder trial of Johnny Pius. The 13-year-old missing boy's body was discovered dead in a wooded area, having been brutally beaten. A neighbor found the boy's body buried under logs, branches, and leaves.

The four boys would eventually be charged with the murder: 14-year-old Michael Quartararo, his 15-year-old brother Peter, 17-year-old Robert Brensic, and 17-year-old Thomas Ryan. The four were neighborhood boys who all knew one another. They were accused of violently beating Johnny then stuffing six stones the size of marbles into the boy's mouth and down his throat, resulting in death via asphyxiation. The boys had no criminal record.

The alleged murder was over a minibike the four had stolen, the police believing that Johnny Pius had witnessed the theft and, therefore, had to be silenced—permanently. That was the police version; the homicide detectives' theory and story. The so-called *confession* was initially spoon-fed to 15-year-old Peter Quartararo by employing in-your-face threats, physical abuse, and other tactics including food deprivation. Full cooperation netted the boy a burger after many hours of intense interrogation.

The minibike had been a broken-down framework worth five bucks at best. To ensure the boy's silence, the foursome purportedly killed Pius, each participating in the thirteen-year-old's death in the back of the Dogwood Elementary School in Smithtown. The four had not been advised of their rights nor were they allowed to make a call home. Peter's *confession* was designed to implicate Michael, Robert, and Thomas as well, for they had lied about stealing the minibike, so it stood to reason that they were also lying about the murder of Johnny Pius—at least in the minds of the police. As mentioned earlier, Peter was given details of the murder then told precisely what to say by Detective Anthony Palumbo. Peter had to be prompted throughout the confession by Palumbo to keep a good part of the *story* straight.

Next, Peter was driven to the crime scene by the detectives, surreptitiously audiotaped to expand on the recorded details the police fed him and wanted him to clarify. Thomas Spota, then head of the Major Offense Bureau listened to the taped *confession*, filled with contradictions and was barely audible. But Spota would work with what he had, a flimsy convoluted *confession*. What the young attorney, Spota, needed next was a witness of sorts. Hence, Jimmy Burke would be Spota's ticket to eventually seal the four boys' fate.

When the mother of the Quartararo boys was finally able to see Peter in the interrogation room at the police precinct, with Detective Palumbo present, she flat-out asked her son, "Did you and Michael help kill the Pius boy?" "Yes," Peter *confessed*. Palumbo then called for the younger brother, Michael, whom the mother had brought back to the station as asked. Palumbo told Michael that his brother Peter had confessed to the murder of Johnny Pius, and that it was now time for him to do likewise. Michael erupted, declaring that he didn't know what Peter was talking about, adding that he never even saw Johnny Pius that night. Peter asked Detective Palumbo if he could speak to his mother alone. As soon as the detective stepped from the interview room, Peter said to his mother, "I didn't do it."

Later that evening, Philip Quartararo, an auxiliary police officer, whose ex-wife had called him earlier, drove to the station and asked the detective to be left alone for a moment with his sons Peter and Michael. Palumbo complied. Philip told the boys that it would be better to tell the truth now. Both boys vehemently denied any knowledge of Johnny's murder. "Then why would you confess to something you didn't do?" the father asked Peter. Peter went on to explain the yelling, the screaming, the threats, the physical abuse of the detective kicking Peter's legs, including the fact that he was starving while undergoing the intense interrogation for many hours. Peter had given the detectives what they wanted to hear to end his horrendous ordeal.

At that point in time, Robert Brensic and Thomas Ryan had no idea what Peter was talking about either, truly nonplused when they heard of what they were being accused. It was bizarre, surreal.

The police investigation into Johnny Pius' murder was absolutely, positively, unequivocally mind-blowing. It was anything but an investigation. It was, in fact, a series of botched attempts to assign blame and elicit a confession. It began with simply a hunch, an assumption, a belief on the part of detectives assigned to the case that at least one of the four boys committed the murder. Forensic analysis was an afterthought, and if it turned out that the scientific evidence contradicted the coerced *confession* that detectives elicited from Peter, well, the torpedoes be damned!

There was a big problem with the physical timeline in the Johnny Pius case referencing the location of where the crime took place and to where the body was dragged off; it did not add up. In fact, there were many problems with the case. The four boys were temporarily released as the case against them was weak at that point.

We will see a similar scenario in the well-documented Martin Tankleff case. These developments happened time and time again. Travesties of justice, pure and simple.

Suffolk County homicide Detectives Thomas Gill and his partner Richard Reck, the lead detectives, failed to properly follow up on the investigation, particularly concerning subsequent interviews with Johnny Pius' parents, whose stories referencing the timeline of Johnny's disappearance from their home that evening had changed dramatically; also, with a troublesome youth who lived across the street: a Robert V. Burke (no relation to Jimmy Burke). Additionally, very little note taking was recorded at the crime scene and in subsequent interviews conducted as it was homicide's policy to muddy the waters to limit the ammunition for the defense team, whose job it is to create reasonable doubt in the jury's mind. A so-called *confession* made a homicide detective's work virtually bulletproof.

At the initial trial, Spota's star witness, Jimmy Burke, testified that Michael Quartararo had told him the reason why he and the other three boys had killed Johnny Pius, saying, "If you were drunk and stoned, and you didn't want to get caught, you would do the same thing." The conversation between Michael Quartararo and Jimmy Burke purportedly took place following John Pius' funeral mass. Burke also testified that Michael Quartararo had told him, "I didn't touch the kid. All I did was put the bike against the tree," referring to Pius' own bike. But the bike had been placed there by a neighbor, referencing the search for Johnny Pius. Burke also said that Robert Brensic told him, "The pigs fucked up and they'll never get me." The jury believed young Jimmy Burke's testimony, and Spota convinced the jury of twelve that the four youths had chased Johnny Pius down, beat and murdered him, believing that Pius would "rat them out" for stealing the minibike.

Peter Quartararo's audiotaped *confession*, secretly recorded in the car before Detectives Anthony Palumbo and his partner Gary Leonard, coupled to Peter's initial *confession* in the interrogation room at the police precinct, compounded by Jimmy Burke's testimony at trial, resulted in the conviction of the four boys.

Interestingly, there had been a potential fly in the ointment for the prosecution from the onset. An 18-year-old boy living directly across the street from the Pius's home had bragged to friends that he, not the four boys, had murdered Johnny Pius. Robert V. Burke stated in sum and substance that, "I shoved my cock in his mouth and he choked on it . . . and no one would know because I shoved stones down the kid's mouth."

That statement should have and did raise a red flag with homicide, especially after learning from an adult confidential source that Robert V. Burke had a very violent temper and history from early on, a history that fit a pattern representative of the way in which Johnny Pius was murdered. After being beaten to the ground, Johnny's face was stomped upon, the imprint of a sneaker indelibly marking his face. The detectives had earlier checked the sneaker patterns of several suspects. Did the detectives bother to check out that important lead concerning Robert V. Burke? No, they had not.

Robert Burke was deemed mentally disturbed by members of his own family and often exhibited extremely violent behavior, at times of a sexual propensity. One time, he rendered a kid unconscious, kicking and stomping the kid's face behind the high school. Was that not reminiscent of Johnny Pius' murder? A school psychologist and a probation officer respectively reported Robert Burke's anti-authority and anti-social behavior. His violence was becoming randomly excessive, yet the detectives did not consider Robert Burke a suspect. He had an alibi for the night of Johnny's murder, saying that he was at a party at his girlfriend's home. The alibi was not checked out until months later, and admittedly not investigated any further by police (when memories begin to fade), then suddenly dropped. Why? The answer: The police had Peter's initial verbal *confession* taken in the interrogation room at the police precinct, then later in the homicide detectives' vehicle, and were steadily building their case for the DA's office.

A private detective for the Ryan family subsequently learned that Robert V. Burke's alibi for the night of Johnny Pius' murder was riddled with holes: contradictions and confusion. The alibi proved unreliable. That still left Peter Quartararo's *confessions*.

Thomas Spota had offered the four boys a deal that would have left them with unblemished adult criminal records. All they had to do was admit to the murder of Johnny Pius and testify to that as fact. The four boys flatly refused. So, the prosecution went with their star *witness*, Jimmy Burke, who would give sworn testimony in court that Michael Quartararo and Robert Brensic had confessed their guilt to him referencing the murder of Johnny Pius. The matter went to several trials over the course of eleven years.

A long story made endless, the four boys, as mentioned, went away to prison for years before the verdicts were eventually overturned.

CHAPTER FIVE

Suffolk County Police Sergeant James Burke (year 1999): referencing Guy Malone and Heather Malone.

In a nonfiction book written about Jimmy Burke published in 2022, *Jimmy the King,* its author, Gus Garcia-Roberts, mentions that he changed the given names of two individuals, that he used pseudonyms in lieu of their actual first names. Also, Garcia-Roberts assigns no surnames, so you are left totally in the dark as to whom he is addressing. I, however, *do not* alter those names in my accounting of the pair in my sequel to ***The Long Island Serial Killer Murders ~ Gilgo Beach and Beyond***, titled ***Snuff Stuff***.

The fictional given names that Garcia-Roberts assigns for those two individuals are Doug and Michelle. They were actually husband and wife, Guy Malone and Heather Malone. Those names are *perhaps* relevant concerning certain factors; namely, photographic evidence regarding the mysterious belt that Geraldine Hart (police cwithout himommissioner of Suffolk County at the time) shared with the public as evidence in the Gilgo Beach murders. The leather belt, not believed to belong to any one of the LISK (**L**ong **I**sland **S**erial **K**iller) victims, suggesting that the belt belonged to the murderer, was found near one of the four bodies on Gilgo Beach. The embossed lettering, depending on which way you held the belt, showed the half-inch high characters depicting the initials W H, or H M. Read into that what you will for the moment.

Scribed in my fictional/nonfictional accounting titled *Snuff Stuff* (written under the umbrella of New Journalism), I interpret the initials H M as assigned to **H**eather **M**alone. It makes for plausible speculation, especially when you consider the fact that Heather Malone lived with James Burke as his mistress, off and on, for considerable periods of time, suggesting that Burke would certainly have had access to her belongings. I am not implying that Heather Malone is a killer, rather that James Burke may be somehow involved in the LISK murders. It is a fact that authorities proffered Burke as a possible suspect. Also, it has been substantially stipulated that James Burke operated a prostitution ring with Heather Malone as evidenced in that the Internal Affairs Bureau was pursuing those allegations relentlessly.

Excerpted from *Snuff Stuff*, I relate the Guy Malone, Heather Malone events via a Frank MacKay podcast interview with Guy Malone on January 23, 2020, discussing his wife, Heather Malone. The story began in January of 1999:

Heather Malone was a hairdresser who cut James Burke's hair. Guy Malone, an insurance salesman, and Heather lived in Smithtown. Burke lived very close by. Heather had asked her husband to go downstairs to get a paperback book from her purse. He does and finds a large gold police badge in her bag along with Detective Sergeant

Burke's business card used as a bookmark. When Guy Malone confronted his wife, she used the customer/hair stylist relationship as her excuse for having those two items. Guy does not push the issue at that point in time.

Guy Malone later tells JVC's talk show host, Frank MacKay, on his nationally syndicated radio program titled *Breaking it Down with Frank MacKay*, that Heather is rarely home at night. Guy is home taking care of their five-year-old daughter, and that when Heather goes out in the evenings, she is dressed to kill. Very sexy. Hot. Tight black skirts, makeup, et cetera, et cetera. Guy and Heather's marital relationship is admittedly rocky to begin with. It seemed very odd that she would send him downstairs to fetch a book from her purse without him realizing that he would at least see the large gold police badge, let alone the detective sergeant's business card used as a bookmarker. It seems like a setup from the get-go, as if she *wanted* him to find those items.

A week and a half later, Guy questions Heather about the detective's badge and business card. An argument ensues. The argument turns physical. She punches him with a powerful blow to his right temple, knocking him to the floor. He lost consciousness for a moment, inadvertently stepping on and bruising her toe when he got up. She calls the police; he's arrested and spends the night in jail. Long story short, Guy's lawyer relates *his client's* side of the story and has Guy show the judge a good size bruise on the side of his temple. A thirty-day cooling off period is ordered by the judge. However, Heather had filed for an order of protection, and Guy was not allowed in his own home for forty some days. Folks who know Guy cannot believe what is happening to this decent fellow. Guy soon learns about a series of very detailed facts relating to Heather's affairs with other men.

So, Guy Malone hires a private investigator. Phone records over the course of a past year reveal many, many communications for the same number; ten to fifteen calls per day, every day, less than a minute long. The phone number goes through to a supposed nail salon of Heather's best friend. But Heather's best friend has no such nail salon business. Then to whom are these phone calls going? Guy learns that the number is an *unlisted* Page Net (short for Paging Network) phone number. The big question is, if it's a nail salon business, why is it an unlisted number? After spending eight hundred dollars for a further investigation because money talks and bullshit walks, Guy learns that the number is registered to a *Jane* Burke at address number 2 Sammis Street in Smithtown. Number 2 Sammis Street is *James* Burke's home address! That address is around the corner from the Malone residence.

Guy Malone had a good friend at Park's Bake Shop, King's Park, Smithtown; a hangout for the cops at the Fourth Precinct. Virtually everyone at the precinct knew about Heather Malone and Sergeant James Burke; Burke's *relationship* and his ties to prostitution. The expensive gifts Heather received from Burke were a Rolex watch, Louis Vuitton luggage (one piece costing eight hundred fifty dollars). The police officers knew Heather was untouchable, protected by Burke. Burke had given Heather eighteen hundred dollars to rent an apartment, covering the lease and security. The apartment had been rented *prior* to Heather and Guy's altercation and arrest, which she had said she rented *after* the fact. It was a lie and proved in court with documentation; that is, lease and rental receipt dates.

Sergeant Jimmy Burke had given Heather Malone a beeper to solicit clients for the purposes of prostitution. Burke now knows that Guy is on to him. Burke and Heather concoct a story of a second assault by her husband at the couple's five-year-old daughter's kindergarten graduation. Guy's second arrest results in a class B felony, which leads to a Grand Jury. In court, the daughter's teacher and two witnesses testify on behalf of Guy that the so-called 'attack' at the school never happened, and Guy was found not guilty. In a turn of events, Heather was found guilty again of lying before a Grand Jury. She's caught in a *big* lie.

Guy files for divorce. In a deposition, James Burke is brought in and questioned by Guy Malone's attorney. Burke denies any connection to prostitution. He's lying through his teeth while under oath. Who is representing Burke? Thomas Spota's law firm. Remarkably, the judge stops the show in mid-stream! He has, quote unquote, "heard enough" and rules in Guy's favor. Guy gets to keep the house. So, Guy's win is a Pyrrhic victory, hollow in the sense that he loses the opportunity through his attorney to question Burke and rip him apart, too, like he had his wife during an EBT (Examination Before Trial), referencing all of Heather's and Burke's lies and deceptions. Guy's attorney had over two hundred questions prepared on a yellow-lined legal pad. Ask yourself what went on behind closed doors for the judge to stop the trial; why stop the trial? The answer is that certain matters would have surfaced about police Sergeant James Burke that were best left alone as far as the powers that be were concerned.

Heather and her five-year-old daughter then lived with Burke for approximately seven years, off and on again for another three. The daughter is now in her late twenties and has nothing to do with her mother from the day she learned the truth. To this day, Guy Malone believes that the disgraced, then Chief of Police James Burke, has intimate knowledge of the Long Island Serial Killer murders—not that he is necessarily a murderer.

And those are just some of the highlights that you can hear for yourself. Simply check out JVC Broadcasting with Frank MacKay interviewing Guy Malone: 103.9 News Radio. Google the 45-minute, 19-second interview. It is surely an eye-opener.

Following these events, Heather Malone, maiden name Volino, was living in Warwick, Rhode Island at the time of this research, listed under numerous aliases and more than a dozen phone numbers. Does that not sound like a familiar pattern? She and another woman, along with Burke had run a prostitution ring not only involving young women, but for the procurement of young boys as well, which fits in with why Burke would have pornographic videos of pubescent boys in his party bag that Christopher Loeb had stolen from Burke's vehicle. More on that other woman in a moment.

CHAPTER SIX

Back in 1995, the Internal Affairs Bureau already knew about Burke's involvement with Lowrita Rickenbacker, a known prostitute who Burke had sex with while on duty, in uniform, and in his police vehicle, whereby he *loses* his service gun on more than one occasion, which she had taken then he later recovered. Lowrita Rickenbacker had the same beeper number that Heather Malone was later given.

Lowrita Rickenbacher

Rickenbacker's police record was sealed. Burke had been busted for prostitution and transferred from the Second Precinct in Huntington to the Fourth Precinct in Smithtown. It was all hush-hush. The public was not privy to this. Thomas Spota was Burke's attorney in these earlier matters. What were the consequences this time around for the detective sergeant referencing Heather Malone and Jimmy Burke's prostitution ring? Burke is promoted to lieutenant. Guy Malone saw red. Internal Affairs kept everything under wraps; they did nothing. So, Guy later brought those pieces of information to light and handed the story to Tanya Lopez of *Newsday*, which was then verified by Lopez. The story ran in part; however, the full-length version got squashed. Guy also gave that and other subsequent information to John Ray, attorney for the Shannan Gilbert estate. John Ray was busy building a circumstantial case that named James Burke and Dr. Peter Hackett as possible suspects in the LISK (**L**ong **I**sland **S**erial **K**iller) murders.

Attorney John Ray

On the night of May 3, 2010, two days after Shannan Gilbert went missing, Peter Hackett had phoned Shannan's mother, Mari, and asked if Shannan had returned home. She had not. He told the woman that he ran a halfway house for troubled youths, took Shannan in that evening after she pounded on his door, gave her a drug to help calm her, and then she left. Hackett later said that he had never called Shannan's mother. Phone records proved otherwise. Hackett was not considered a suspect.

Nineteen months later, the police recovered Shannan Gilbert's body from a marshy area behind Peter Hackett's home; he was still not considered a suspect. One detective said of the retired Suffolk County emergency services doctor that ". . . he likes to get himself involved and has a history of injecting himself into media attention-grabbing events." Another detective echoed the same refrain, adding, "We believe that Peter Hackett called the mother as a show of support and to sincerely offer any assistance." That was Detective Dominick Varrone, Chief of Detectives, Suffolk County Police Department, Yaphank.

Interestingly, there is a strong connection between Peter Hackett and James Burke referencing the airline disaster near East Moriches back in the late nineties in which two hundred thirty people were killed. I'm referring to the TWA Flight 800 crash to which both Burke and Hackett had been assigned. Years later, both men in separate interviews claimed that the most memorable moment of their career with the police was in dealing with the recovery of those bodies. The two had worked together closely. Doctor Peter C. Hackett of Oak Beach was and is the wild card in the disappearance of Shannan Gilbert.

The search for Shannan Gilbert had led to the discovery of the first four young women (dubbed the Gilgo Four), all sex workers, who advertised their services through Craigslist, and whose remains were found wrapped in burlap, their bodies dumped like trash along Ocean Parkway. Only then did the police acknowledge that they had a serial killer in their midst. As time marched on, several other bodies (and/or their remains) were found along that long and narrow stretch of thick, thorny underbrush running parallel between Ocean Parkway and area beaches bordering Suffolk and Nassau counties on Long Island: a dumping ground for those victims.

Yet the initial finding of the Suffolk County medical examiner's autopsy stated that the cause of Shannan's death was undetermined. As previously mentioned, an independent autopsy performed by renowned pathologist, Michael Baden, hired by the Gilbert family, determined that the cause of Shannan's death was consistent with strangulation. Shannan's hyoid bone had been compromised. Police, however, still speculate to this very day that her death was an accident, that she had *probably* drowned—what the police are still calling a "misadventure." What happened to Shannan Gilbert after that early morning hour is *seemingly* shrouded in mystery. What happened to Shannan Gilbert during that early morning hour is that she was very likely murdered by the Long Island Serial Killer, or killers!

A piece of trivia referencing the hyoid bone: The hyoid bone is a U-shaped bone at the roof of the tongue that has no contact with any other bone in the human body.

The criminal investigation by the Internal Affairs Bureau (IAB) into Burke's Smithtown prostitution ring, purportedly operated with Lowrita Rickenbacker and later Heather Malone, was active and ongoing, headed by the former chief of the IAB department, Philip Robilotto. District Attorney Spota made the whole messy matter go away, addressing the situation with Robert Kearon, Bureau Chief/District Attorney's Office. Spota wrote to him:

> Dear Bob,
>
> Please keep this file confidential, and do not disclose its contents to anybody else in this office.

The message was made very clear and to the point. Detective Lieutenant James C. Burke was untouchable. Phil Robilotto admitted defeat. Quote: "When you got the District Attorney in your pocket like Burke did, you weren't going to get much done against him." Unquote. Phil put in his papers, retiring to Florida.

CHAPTER SEVEN

A young Jimmy Burke had expressed early on to his childhood friends that he wanted to become a cop, not because he wanted to serve and protect, "but because he wanted to get away with breaking the law," said Mike Quartararo of his best friend at the time. "Jimmy was an extremely bright boy, a brilliant bullshitter, who enjoyed, like most of his friends, to drink beer and smoke pot," many a source inclusive of Mike Quartararo has said in sum and substance.

After helping to win a victory for Thomas Spota via Jimmy's court testimony at the trial of the four defendants charged with the murder of Johnny Pius, Jimmy was on his way to becoming a cop. Spota helped Jimmy climb the ladder from a beat cop to the chief of police of one of the largest police forces in the country: the Suffolk County Police Department. By then, Spota was solidly implanted as the Suffolk County District Attorney. However, Jimmy Burke's rise to power was not without bumps along the way. But Spota and his people were always there to help smooth the way for Jimmy, dealing with several serious problems that he had created for himself.

Suffolk County Executive Steve Bellone was warned ahead of time of the dangers of making James Burke police chief, but Bellone did not heed those warnings. In an early phone conversation with one of the editors from *Newsday*, Bellone stated that he knew Burke was a quote unquote sociopath. Nonetheless, Burke was promoted to chief of police. Later, Bellone denied having made that statement to the *Newsday* editor by conveniently failing to remember the conversation. It begs the question as to why Bellone did not fire Burke earlier in time. Bellone knew Burke's track record from the onset. Then there came a point where everyone knew that District Attorney Thomas

Spota and his top aide, Christopher McPartland, were to protect Jimmy Burke at all cost.

Suffolk County Executive Steve Bellone

Jimmy Burke never married, and there are no children of record. However, it is rumored that he fathered a love child with known prostitute Lowrita Rickenbacker. A son. Supposedly, there is a remarkable resemblance to Jimmy. Subjective, I realize, but worth mentioning.

Back in the 90s, Patrick Cuff, former Suffolk County police commander, led an internal affairs investigation into Jimmy Burke, the then sergeant who was caught having sex with Lowrita Rickenbacker in his patrol car while on duty. After being made chief of police in 2012, Burke went after Patrick Cuff with a vengeance, retaliation for the internal affairs investigation into him and Lowrita Rickenbacker. Burke brought the wrath of God down on Patrick Cuff. Cuff was demoted four ranks and sent off to work in a property warehouse.

Earlier in time, Patrick Cuff's 18-year-old son had been seen outside his home with his father's handgun. Christopher McPartland of Spota's office immediately tried to upgrade Cuff's son's charges from a misdemeanor to a felony. The cops who knew McPartland feared his power, referring to him among themselves as "The Lord of Darkness."

The "Administration," as they referred to themselves, was comprised of District Attorney Thomas Spota, his chief aide of the Anti-Corruption Bureau, Christopher McPartland, and the appointed chief of police, James Burke. The trio ruled the roost. Birds of a feather. Burke never believed that Christopher Loeb's allegations of being beaten would be believed. Certainly not the word of a convicted drug addict over the word and world of a decorated soul such as he: Chief of Police James Burke. Not in a million years. In a court settlement, Christopher Loeb was awarded $1.5 million dollars. Spota and McPartland never fathomed that their reign would end in ruination.

Former Suffolk County Executive Steven Levy

In 2010, what kind of dirt did Thomas Spota have on then County Executive Steve Levy to force him to leave office at the end of his term, paving the way for Steve Bellone to be appointed as the new county executive in Levy's stead? The reported reason was not what it seemed. Ostensibly, it was over Levy's mishandling of campaign funds. The real ammunition for having gotten rid of Steve Levy was coming to light. The leverage Spota held was a smear tactic: the threat to reveal one of Levy's aide as a homosexual. Spota, Burke, and McPartland had hatched a plot to bring about that very result. Levy, in an undisclosed agreement, turned over his campaign war chest of $4 million to Spota. Ironically, as it would later be disclosed, it was a case of one pot calling the other kettle black.

In reality, Burke wielded more power than either Spota or McPartland in that the chief of police had discretionary control and power. In other words, Burke could do what he damn well pleased, whereas Spota and McPartland had to work within the set parameters of the law. And then that seemingly impenetrable wall started to tumble down around them. Next step, damage control. Burke was dealt with rather effectively. Agree to a plea deal or face an inevitable possibility of a trial and many more years behind bars. Steve Bellone simply claimed that he had been duped, that he had no knowledge the man he hired, Burke, was a sociopath.

Postponement after postponement. Excuse after excuse. Covid was a blessing for the defense team's attorneys and their clients. It bought them lots of time. Presenting the pair, Thomas Spota and Christopher McPartland, as ". . . broken men whose lives have been shattered, their clients were not deserving of imprisonment for the cover-up of the Christopher Loeb beating," the team had argued. After all, "It was Burke who did the beating, not Spota or McPartland," the team continued to argue. "The district attorney and his aide were only trying to protect their guy, James Burke, a decorated cop, a man who had gone after known heroin addict Christopher Loeb, who had, indeed, gone into Chief of Police Burke's unlocked department-issued black 2008 GMC Yukon vehicle and stole personal property from the backseat." The duffel bag. Some defense.

The duffel bag was humorously referred to as the chief's "party bag," containing Burke's gun belt, ammunition, box of cigars, bottle of Viagra, sex toys, sex videos, along with a plethora of pornography—some of homosexual content involving pubescent boys. Subsequently revealed was that the duffel bag also contained a snuff video, coupled to the fact, and corroborated by several prostitutes and partygoers, that Burke was into rough sex. Burke's real crime in the mind's eye of Spota and McPartland was getting caught. Getting caught was the crime, not the crime itself. Getting caught, accused, found guilty, and sentenced was the shame of it all.

Police Chief Jimmy Burke had successfully kept the feds at arm's length during the LISK investigation for several years, not only to deflect attention away from the Christopher Loeb debacle, but to divert attention away from the Gilgo Beach/Oak Beach matter at hand. Thomas Spota and his aide Christopher McPartland covered up Burke's mess for three years, not only to protect Spota's buddy from a federal investigation, but to ensure that the spotlight was not on the Gilgo Beach/Oak Beach matter. Why? The answer is because the area was a playground for Jimmy Burke and a group of very powerful Nassau and Suffolk Counties elite, comprised of his friends and partygoers.

In 2012, newly appointed police chief Jimmy Burke had dismantled the otherwise unquestionably successful Unit Task Force operations performed by Suffolk County detectives John Oliva and William Maldonado in combating MS-13, the notorious Salvadorian gang that had gained a solid foothold in the heavily populated Latino neighborhoods of Central Islip and Brentwood. Why? Again, the answer is because Burke, Spota, and McPartland wanted to rid the county of a hovering FBI presence. The Bureau was probing several areas of interest concerning Thomas Spota, Jimmy Burke, and Christopher McPartland in connection to cover-ups. FBI agents were clandestinely looking into the Long Island Serial Killer murders.

Suffolk County Police Detective John Oliva was one of the good guys who tried to warn the public of The Administration's crimes by leaking information to *Newsday*. As the result of a wiretap that the district attorney's office had placed on Oliva's phone, the leak was revealed. Burke fired Oliva for misconduct, which resulted in a conditional discharge. The charge would normally have amounted to a misdemeanor; however, the matter was conducted as a serious criminal act—just one of many of The Administration's retaliatory moves and measures. Insiders wondered if then interim District Attorney Tim Sini would correct that egregious wrong before he left office in January. Oliva and his partner had done outstanding work concerning MS-13. Both he and his partner Willie Maldonado were specifically singled out and targeted by the gang via contracts put on the detectives' heads.

When Oliva was interviewed by journalist Alexis Linkletter (*Unraveled* documentary) as to why Jimmy Burke thwarted the LISK investigation from the onset, Oliva responded: "Burke may have skeletons in the closet."

Days before Thomas Spota and Christopher McPartland would surrender to authorities, Suffolk County District Attorney Timothy D. Sini stated that the Conviction Integrity Bureau (CIB) dismissed the criminal charges brought against Detective John Oliva.

Detective John Oliva

John Ray, attorney for the Shannan Gilbert and Jessica Taylor families, has publicly stated that he believes Peter Hackett is responsible for

Shannan Gilbert's death, not that he necessarily murdered her. Others in law enforcement also believe that Jimmy Burke is a suspect in the LISK murders.

Lieutenant James Hickey was on the fringe of the "Administration's Inner Circle," as they cavalierly referred to themselves, that being the tyrannical trio: Burke, Spota, and McPartland; that is, up until the time Hickey turned tail and testified against the three in federal court, referencing the Jimmy Burke cover-up beating of Christopher Loeb.

Lieutenant James Hickey

On October 19, 2021, a debate was moderated by *Newsday's* associate editor Joye Brown, between the incumbent district attorney Tim Sini and Ray Tierney the challenger. The November 2nd election for district attorney of Suffolk County was two weeks away. The 1 hour, 3 minute, 52 second broadcast that evening was headlined: **Tim Sini, Ray Tierney tangle at Newsday Town Hall for Suffolk district attorney race**.

Left: Suffolk County District Attorney Raymond Tierney
Right: Former Suffolk County District Attorney Timothy Sini

In short, the two candidates referred to each other as prevaricators. It was not until the last four minutes of the debate that the Gilgo Beach murders and Oak Beach investigation were discussed. One question addressed the release of the Shannan Gilbert 911 tapes, which Sini was initially opposed to but later did a one-eighty. Tierney brought up the fact that the FBI was held at arm's length from investigating the Long Island Serial Killer case, but Sini deflected that point, stating that when he was brought in as district attorney, he reached out to the FBI and brought agent Geraldine Hart into the picture, who became Suffolk County police commissioner. But airtime did not allow for Tierney to refute the fact that Geraldine Hart was no longer the police commissioner and to get to crux of the matter: Why was the LISK investigation thwarted under Spota's watch?

The "why" was one of the questions from New York State Senator Phil Boyle, along with another. Why was his request for an investigation into the matter ignored? Keep firmly in mind that initially the feds were not allowed to touch the crime scene reports or view the photographs. Absolutely astonishing!

Senator Phil Boyle

Sini went on to say how diligently Suffolk County homicide was working to solve the case, while Tierney pointed out that was not the case at all, that the experienced homicide detectives had been taken off the case and that assistants from the district attorney's office were handling the matter, further stating Sini's approach was a disaster. And that was that. Four minutes left to discuss one of the nation's most notorious murder case(s) in the annals of homicidal history—stemming from the Suffolk County district attorney's office.

How the chief of police and the district attorney's office, under Spota, got away with keeping the FBI out of the LISK investigation and the reasons why was, indeed, astonishing. Credit for the explanation goes to Greg Blass, a six-term county legislator who wrote an article for the RiverheadLOCAL.com opinion column, dated October 17, 2021. I'll excerpt a passage from Blass' article.

> "That a police chief can remove the FBI from a murder investigation in itself boggles the mind. It's something to do with "initial jurisdiction" and other bureaucratic gibberish, and who calls the shots. Why would he [Burke] do this — and why did his civilian superiors allow it?"

That single paragraph succinctly raises a series of serious questions. "Initial jurisdiction." As far as Blass' last two questions were concerned, James Burke was protecting himself, as were his cronies—protecting himself from the fact that he was a possible suspect in the murder of young women as it pertained to the Long Island Serial Killer case, the least of which was the Christopher Loeb matter. Burke referred to those cops surrounding him as his "Palace Guard."

Keep in mind what Police Chief James Burke had done. He and Detectives Kenneth Bombace, Anthony Leto, along with other detectives, brutally beat Christopher Loeb while handcuffed to an eyebolt fastened to the floor in the interrogation room. Burke lost it when Loeb called him a pedophile. They punched him repeatedly in the head and ribs for better than a quarter of an hour. They choked him till he lost consciousness. They threatened to kill him with an overdose of heroin, what police refer to as a "hot shot." They threatened to arrest and rape his mother. They held him for 48 hours while refusing his requests for a lawyer. Spota, McPartland, and Burke covered it up.

Let's also examine a few facts that many folks don't know, and those who do tend to lose sight in short order: Legally, Police Chief James Burke had no business showing up at the Loeb residence in the first place. Why? Because Burke's the *victim* of the crime; that is, the stolen duffel bag. Before Burke arrived, police officers were at Loeb's home along with a member of the Suffolk County Police Intelligence Section. Detective Thomas Cottingham and his partner Kenneth Regensburg had been called to the Smithtown home. Cottingham was the lead investigator on the case. The home was searched. A second search had been conducted. Christopher Loeb's probation officer, Francine Ruggiero, was also present. Nothing had been logged or inventoried at that point, Ruggiero later testified in court. Burke pulls into Loeb's driveway with his GMC Yukon vehicle from which Christopher Loeb swiped the chief's party bag. Burke enters the home and grabs the duffel bag, property of a crime scene but is never entered into evidence. Of course, we know the reasons why: embarrassment to outright humiliation being *chief* among the least of the police chief's concerns.

Eventually, Suffolk County Detectives James Hickey, Kenneth Bombace, Anthony Leto, Thomas Cottingham, Christopher Nealis, Kenneth Regensburg, Keith Sinclair, along with Police Officer Brian Draiss and Sergeant Michael Kelly, flipped on and testified against their chief, who ruined the lives of so many.

CHAPTER EIGHT

Leading up to the days of Jimmy Burke's undoing, two days after Shannan Gilbert's body was discovered, Police Chief James Burke gave Chief of Detectives Dominick Varrone and other high-ranking officials involved in the LISK investigation an ultimatum: "Within 15 days, put in your retirement papers or be demoted to the rank of captain," quote unquote. This would have had a detrimental effect referencing their pensions and other retirement benefits had they remained on the job. The men were not debriefed, neither then or at a later point—never asked to offer input to bring the next investigative team up to speed referencing the LISK murders. In other words, the passing of the baton was purposely dropped.

Additional Facts:

- Early on in his career, Suffolk County police officer Robert Trotta had been asked by then Sergeant James Burke if he could get him a snuff film. At the time, Officer Trotta did not even know what a snuff film was. Burke went on to explain in graphic detail how the body of a dying murder victim reacts, elaborating in a physiological sense as to how the murderous act sexually arouses the perpetrator.

Current Suffolk County Legislator Robert Trotta

- Attorney John Ray relates the story of a police officer who describes an incident referencing James Burke's behavior when viewing a snuff film for police training purposes. Burke is giggling hysterically as to what was horrifically unfolding in the film.

- According to a detective and several women attending an after-hours restaurant party for firemen and police, Burke is playing around with a necktie, simulating the strangulation of one of the stripper/sex workers present.

- In August 2011, four months into the nineteen months before Shannan Gilbert's remains are found, 'Leanne' [actual name withheld], attorney John Ray's witness in a sworn statement says that James Burke is at a cocaine-fueled sex party in Oak Beach. She performs oral sex on Burke in the bathroom of the home. He is *extremely* rough with her.

- Property records referencing the residence where 'Leanne' attended that sex party is the property which has ties to individuals who work in the highest ranks of Suffolk County government. The home is but a few miles away from the serial killer(s) dumping grounds; i.e., Gilgo Beach.

- Suffolk County District Attorney Tim Sini at the time, says that "James Burke is "proffered" (meaning considered) a suspect" in the LISK investigation.

- Longtime local Oak Beach resident Joe Scalise went on record as stating that "Oak Beach is a den of debauchery."

- Christopher Loeb's updated story, in an interview with journalist Billy Jensen (*Unraveled* podcast), named additional items of a sexual nature found in Chief of Police James Burke's 'party bag': a pink butt plug, anal beads, lubricants, stack of five or six pornographic DVDs. One is wrapped with a white covering. Loeb puts it into a DVD player for about two minutes. "I saw a guy with a mask on torturing a girl," Loeb says. "Her hands were tied behind her back. Her make-up was running down her face. She was scared to death. It looked like they were going to kill her." That's the snuff film to which Loeb refers.

- When people who knew James Burke well were asked if the police chief could be the serial killer, a former police officer and a once good friend of Burke's succinctly stated, "He has that vibe."

- When Rob Trotta, now a Suffolk County Legislator, was asked the same question, he related a story. Trotta had asked that very same question of a federal prosecutor. "Could Burke have killed those girls?" The prosecutor replied, "Probably not all of them."

- In May of 2020, attorney John Ray finally got to hear the 911 recording(s) (plural – having been transferred over to another operator), but with conditions attached by the Suffolk County police. Ray is limited as to what he can say to the public. John Ray and Detective Vincent Stephan report very different interpretations of Shannan's tone played on the tape. Stephan says Shannan was calm during the 911 calls. Ray says, "Outrageously false." Stephan says she was not speaking as if she were in any danger. John Ray says, "Grossly false." Ray says that Stephan is obviously lying about having listened to the tape or lying about what he heard. When Stephan was asked in an interview with journalist Billy Jensen about the discrepancies in his interpretation of the 911 tape, Stephan said, "I stand by what I said in *Newsday*."

- Police claim Shannan Gilbert was not a victim of foul play but that she died of a "misadventure," that is, exposed to the elements and likely drowned. Then why was the 911 tape being withheld from the public for some nine years, since Shannan's death was not considered part of the ongoing Gilgo Beach/Oak Beach investigation? Shannan Gilbert was, indeed, screaming after she ran from the client's home. "They're (plural) trying to kill me!" Who's they? Michael Pak and/or Joseph Brewer? It appears that Michael Pak was the last person to see Shannan alive. At times, Shannan kept her voice silent or low when speaking with one of the 911 operators because she was apparently trying to hide from her pursuer(s): Joseph Brewer (the client) and/or Michael Pak (her escort driver). Detective Vincent Stephan seemingly suffered from selective memory when listening to the 911 recording.

- It is interesting to note, too, that one of the 911 recordings had been taped over, for it had taken months before the Suffolk County police made the connection between the call from Shannan Gilbert on the night she disappeared and a missing person report filed by her family in New Jersey.

Michael Pak

- After the news conference that John Ray and 'Leanne' had given, rumors flew about like a flock of birds in erratic flight. The acronym, **LISK**—**L**ong **I**sland **S**erial **K**iller—was linked to Burke as well as those friends who were close to him; namely, Peter Hackett. Hence, the acronym, LISK, was expanded to LISK**S**, plural—Long Island Serial Killer**s**, for many folks firmly believed, and still do, that there is more than one serial killer responsible for the murders, especially when it was learned that several of the victims were dismembered. The head, hands, and right foot of one woman's body were discovered in proximity to Gilgo Beach, her torso found earlier in time back in Manorville, a hamlet in the northeast corner in the town of Riverhead, a distance of 47 miles.

- It was later learned through genetic genealogy analysis that a Jane Doe was identified as Valerie Mack. According to police, Valerie Mack was never reported missing. In fact, that is not accurate. The New Jersey police would not file a missing person report for Valerie's parents because of Valerie's promiscuous history. Two serial killers, perhaps more, working in concert, was but one of the many theories being bandied about.

- In addition to the discovery of the Gilgo Beach and Manorville victims, the remains of several other young women turned up in Hempstead Lake Park, Mamaroneck, Bellmore, Fire Island, and Lattington (an incorporated village in the town of Oyster Bay, Nassau County). One mutilated body was found in a suitcase, another in a Rubbermaid container, while other bodies were found wrapped in burlap, erroneously speculated as perhaps having originated from the Bissett Nursery in Holtsville, owned by James Bissett, a wealthy developer and co-owner of the Long Island Aquarium and Exhibition Center, in addition to the adjacent Hyatt Place Hotel in the heart of downtown Riverhead.

James Bissett

- Shortly before Christmas in 2011, Jim Bissett committed suicide in his vehicle at Veteran's Memorial Park in Mattituck—a day or two after Shannan Gilbert's body was found by police. Some folks question whether it was, indeed, a suicide. Gilbert's phone number was purportedly listed in Bissett's cellphone directory. An undisputed fact was that Jimmy Bissett and James Burke were very good friends. Savvy folks were beginning to connect the dots. Coincidentally, the same initials referencing some of the key players presented a curious conundrum: **J**oseph **B**rewer, **J**ames **B**urke, **J**immy **B**issett, and **J**ohn **B**ittrolff**.** Keep that last name firmly in mind.

If one is of the belief that there are no coincidences, then one can have a field day with the facts. After summing up the similarities referencing those initials, an award-winning crime-thriller novelist/outdoors writer from Riverhead coined the phrase (shared strictly among friends, of course): "The Good Ol' Boys **J.B.** Sex Club," alluding to the circle of suspicious characters. Yes, that was me!

- A year and a half after Jimmy Bisset's *supposed* suicide, Robert Lanieri, age 60, a food service executive for the Long Island Aquarium, committed suicide at his home in Jamesport.

He hanged himself. Strange connection.

- The Johnny Pius murder case and subsequent trials of defendants Michael Quartararo, Peter Quartararo, Thomas Ryan, and Robert Brensic were the beginning of Thomas Spota and James Burke's long-lasting friendship. There are those who speculate to this very day that their unusually close relationship (of some 42 years) was something more than just mentor and protégé (a 24-year difference in age between them notwithstanding)—or the fact that Spota had groomed Burke from a beat cop to the chief of police while protecting and covering for him in several scandalous situations along the way.

CHAPTER NINE

To expand upon the perpetual Culture of Corruption referencing Suffolk County law enforcement, particularly as it pertains to corrupt detectives and public officials such as Thomas Spota, let's digress for a moment to examine the Martin Tankleff Case referencing the September 7, 1988 murders of his adoptive parents, Seymour and Arlene Tankleff, residing at 33 Seaside Drive, Belle Terre, Port Jefferson.

The couple could not have children. Seymour had testicular cancer. Arlene had a hysterectomy. Sharie Tankleff (married name Sharie Mistretta) is the daughter from Seymour's first wife, Viga. A cast of characters listed below will help you keep track as the incidents unfold. The narrative will be abridged in a bulleted format for the sake of expediency. If one wishes to peruse the 593-page unabridged version, I encourage you to read Richard Firstman and Jay Salpeter's *A Criminal Injustice*.

Cast of Characters (Nonfictional)

Martin Tankleff, age 17, adopted at birth, 1971.

Ron and Carol Falbee, Marty's cousins. Ron, executor of estate and legal guardian.

Sharie (Rother) Mistretta, Marty's stepsister, daughter of Seymour by first marriage.

Seymour M. Tankleff and Arlene, Marty's parents. Seymour retired insurance agent, very wealthy.

Mark Perrone, Marty's best friend.

Macella Falbee, Arlene Tankleff's sister.

Jennifer Johnson, Marty's cousin.

Homicide Detectives K. (for Kevin) James McCready and Norman Rein.

Myron (Mike) Fox, family attorney.

Sergeant Doyle, Detective McCready's boss.

Robert Gottlieb, Marty's first defense attorney.

Jennifer Johnsen, Marty's cousin.

Norman Tankleff, Seymour Tankleff's brother.

Clinton Correctional facility, outside of Plattsburgh, New York, in the village of Dannemora, is the maximum-security prison where Marty was incarcerated.

- Marty's side of story: Marty woke up shortly before 6 a. m., first day of his senior year of high school. It was odd that all lights were on throughout the house.

- Layout of home: Marty's bedroom is located at one end of home. To the right, master bedroom is located across the hallway. Main area of home; front door is open. Ranch style home. Office is located at the other end of home. From Marty's bedroom, he looks in master bedroom. He does not see his mother who is lying dead on the other side of the bed.

- Marty continues past living room and kitchen, on the way to his father's office. He notes that the greenhouse door is open, which leads to office area. Seymour is sitting in a chair at his desk, bloody and gagging for air. Marty calls 911 at 6:14 a.m. Operator instructs Marty to apply pressure with clean towel and to lay Seymour down on the floor, if possible, feet elevated. "Ambulance is on its way."

- Marty returns to his room to get towel and a pillow from another area. Returns to office to get his dad out of chair. Marty lifted or pulled his father out; he is not sure. Elevates his father's feet with pillow, applies pressure with towel over wound.

- Goes from room to room, then to the garage to see if the cars are there; they are. Marty went back into his parents' bedroom, then discovered his mother on the other side of the bed, dead.

- 6:15 a.m. Marty calls Sharie, Marty's stepsister. "Get over here," he says. "What's the matter?" "Something happened to my parents." "What happened?" "Don't know." "Be more specific." "I think they're dead!" Sharie thought Marty was sleepwalking, imagining the whole thing. Marty repeats for her to get over here then hangs up.

- Marty calls best friend and relates what he knows.

- Marty knocks on neighbor's door. Thirty seconds later a police car drives up; three police officers secure the scene. Area is taped off. A short time later, Marty is questioned by Detectives K. James McCready and Norman Rein. Marty immediately said he knows who did this. "My father's business partner, Jerry Steuerman." Steuerman owed Seymour lots of money. Steuerman owned Strathmore Bagels. Marty explains their business relationship was deteriorating.

- Card game the night before went on till 3 a.m. Steuerman stayed behind to discuss business. A heated argument ensued regarding the bagel business arrangement.

- Ambulance arrives 6:25 a.m.

- Marty is a suspect based on evidence detectives immediately saw and the story Marty told, according to McCready. Marty was directed 150–200 feet away from his home near a neighbor's home.

- Seymour Tankleff is transported to Mather Hospital, transferred to University Hospital. [He was in a coma and had died a week later].

- Arrival of family attorney Myron "Uncle Mike" Fox. McCready has conversation with Fox a distance away from Marty, explaining that they are interviewing Marty. Fox said he's heading to the hospital and claims he told McCready at that time that he represented Marty. McCready says that is a lie. He said Fox *later* told him that he represented Marty at around 1:20 p.m., and that all questioning had stopped. [So, who is lying?]

- Marty tells McCready and Rein that he wants to go to the hospital to see his dad. Marty said McCready said, "We'll take you there." McCready denies Marty ever asked that, or asked how his father was doing.

- Marty realizes during travel that the route was not the way to the hospital. Marty was told they were on their way to police headquarters in Yaphank to get a statement from him. "We'll take you to the hospital later. We need info on Jerry Steuerman."

- Marty is in the corner of the 8 x 8-foot interrogation room. Detective Rein is on one side of Marty. He had his hands on Marty's knees and shoulders to comfort him, then at other times he was screaming and yelling at Marty. McCready, on the other side of a desk, was screaming and yelling at Marty, too. They said, "…enough of this already. We know you did it. Just tell us. That's all we need to hear." There were others in the room. Sgt. Doyle threw Marty up against the wall.

- McCready relates ruse as to how he tricked Marty to "*confess*." McCready said Marty's father was pumped full of adrenaline, came out of a coma, and said it was you who did it. Marty denies. "No way. I didn't do anything."

- There comes a point where Marty tells the police what they want to hear. Why? When he was later asked, Marty said, "A way to escape the confines of that environment. It wasn't the truth. They wanted to hear lies. I told them what they wanted to hear." McCready bragged that Marty fell for it. Seymour never came out of a coma.

- The police told Marty they had conducted a humidity test that showed he had taken a shower to clean off the blood.

- Robert Gottlieb, Marty's initial defense attorney.

- Sharie, Marty's stepsister, said she received a call from Marty at either police headquarters in Yaphank or county jail in Yaphank. "I need you to be with me," Marty said." "Did you tell them you did this?" "Yes." "Why?" "I had to. They made me."

- Jennifer Johnsen, Marty's cousin, and Norman Tankleff, Seymour Tankleff's brother stated, "Inconceivable that it could have been Marty." Ron Falbee, Marty's legal guardian, states, "From Marty's physical strength, no way. Impossible."

- Robert Gottlieb, Marty's initial lawyer. "Confession is not truthful. There is no forensic evidence to support Marty did these brutal murders."

- Detective McCready says, "Marty went to open garage door looking for his mother *after* assisting his bloodied father, yet no blood was found on the garage door. Goes to his bedroom to turn the light switch on. Blood is on the wall near light switch. How does blood get on the wall but not the door knob when he would need to unlock the deadbolt to get to the garage?"

- An unnamed member of Suffolk County Police Department, a sergeant of 23 years, relates what McCready and other homicide squad member's tactics were back in '88 re the Tankleff case. "McCready did what he had to do, what was needed to get a confession. McCready did not follow through with the investigation the way you normally would." In other words, when homicide *believed* they had a guilty person, that was it, period.

- McCready: "We don't arrest and charge innocent people."

- Robert Gottlieb: "So clear that Marty is innocent. It's what the police thought/believed happened that Marty must have taken a shower to wash away all the blood from his body, wiped away blood from so-called murder weapons (knife, dumbbell, dumbbell bar). After police first surmise all of this, then having Marty 'confess' to whatever the police wanted him to confess to later. No blood is found in any crevice on bathroom tile, nor in the drain trap, which was removed by forensics. No trace of human tissue, hair, blood. All negative. Nothing."

- The police claim Marty, naked, took a watermelon knife from the kitchen, entered mother's bedroom, where he stabbed and bludgeoned her to death while she was dozing. He walked through the house where he also bludgeoned and stabbed his father to death, then went into the shower and washed away any trace of blood and tissue from knife, dumbbell bar, and himself with a loofah sponge.

- Robert Gottlieb points out others who should have been considered suspects by the police, those who potentially had motive because of the many business deals in which Seymour Tankleff was involved. Yet the police rushed to judgment re Marty.

- Gross lack of evidence and questions pointed in another direction.

- Ron Falbee refers to a bloody copy of a demand note typed out to Jerry Steuerman found on Seymour's desk in his study. It was sent special delivery to Steuerman, care of Strathmore Bagels, 4088 Nesconset Highway, East Setauket. Sent 6/29/88; received 6/30/88.

- Murders occurred on 9/7/88; two months and 7 days after demand note sent to Jerry Steuerman by Seymour Tankleff.

- Sharie, Marty's stepsister, says Seymour and Jerry Steuerman were close, then wouldn't talk. They had a back-and-forth relationship, then toward the end not a very good relationship.

- McCready says Steuerman borrowed money from Seymour to buy equipment to open satellite bagel stores.

- Seymour had gone to pick up checks from Jerry Steuerman at bagel store, and they had gotten into a heated argument. Jerry verbally and physically attacks Seymour in front of customers at store. "You have a chattel on my equipment, my stores, not me. You want to own me, you bastard."

- Robert Gottlieb explains how the murder could have taken place. Between the rooms, master bedroom and office, carpeted in white, there is no blood. No blood on tile flooring. Two or more people enter from each *end* of the house, commit the murders of Arlene and Seymour, exit house same way they entered, not having to trapse *through* the house.

- A week after the murders, Jerry Steuerman stages his own abduction and death and disappears, initially to California. Changes his identity, shaves beard, has his hairpiece rewoven, wears contact lenses. Two weeks later, police find him. Jerry *must* be a suspect, but McCready says no. Police have never considered him to be a suspect. One day after the murders, before he fled, Steuerman withdraws 15K from a joint business account he had with Seymour and Arlene Tankleff. McCready, Rein, and ADA Edward C. Jablonski track Steuerman down in Florida.

- The trio works to prove Steuerman is not the murderer, according to McCready, because of public opinion re Steuerman's actions.

- Marty out on one-million-dollar bail: June 1990; after 2 years, trial is set. After eight days of deliberation, the jury found Marty guilty of his parents' murder. Main reason, many say, is that he displayed no emotion during trial. Receives 50 to life, at which point Marty breaks down and sobs.

- Sharie, Marty's stepsister, now believes Marty is guilty. Only one in the family to believe so. Why? Sharie contested her father's (Seymour's) will; 80% of monies had been left to Marty, 10% to Sharie, 10% to college endorsement fund at Hofstra.

- Sharie had said earlier to Marty: "Marty, we have to talk about this. This is not right." She said Marty said, "It's all mine." "I wanted to choke him. He's not part of this family; he was *brought* into this family."

- Digger O'Dells Restaurant/Bar controversy, Riverhead, Long Island. It is purported that Sharie went into business with Detective James McCready. She said her ex-husband did, but it was her money that financed construction of Digger O'Dells. A bartender friend of McCready's enters into the picture. Bartender friend is friends with Sharie's ex-husband, Ron Rother. McCready said Sharie had nothing to do with the business, that they were not partners.

- Sister of Arlene Tankleff: Marianne McClure. "How can my nephew get 50 years to life? It's surreal. I have hope and will continue to fight for Marty as long as we have to."

- Robert Gottlieb says that ultimately the truth will come out.

- Tankleff's attorneys spent nearly a decade appealing his conviction. By 2000, the only hope is that new evidence would clear Marty. An inmate recommends that retired NYPD Detective Jay Salpeter look into Marty's case. Salpeter learns the case was never properly investigated. Jay tells Marty, if you're innocent, I'll work till I get you out. After a 3-year investigation, Jay Salpeter says he cracked the case.

- Going back to the day of Marty's arraignment, he was being held at the Riverhead Correctional Facility. Ron Falbee and his mother, Marcella (Micky) Falbee, met with Marty in the visiting room. Ron asked Marty straightaway, "Did you do it?" "No, I didn't," Marty answered.

- Marcella (Micky) told Marty to open his shirt. Marty started to open his shirt partway. "All the way," she insisted, to which

Marty complied. Marcella carefully inspected his neck, torso, stomach, and arms. "Turn around." There was not a scratch on her nephew's upper body. Yet, Marty was supposed to have violently attacked and stabbed his mother, Arlene, who, as it was determined by her autopsy, had fought back viciously and mightily.

- When Ron Falbee and Mike McClure (Arlene Tankleff's brother-in-law) went to the morgue to identify Seymour and Arlene's bodies, Mike said, "We saw enough to know that she put up a hell of a battle. Nobody was going to kill Arlene easily." Ron said, "Everything about Arlene was tough—her personality, her size, her strength. It was who she was. Whoever did this would have looked like he went through a war."

- There was unquestionably the size and weight of both Seymour and Arlene to consider against that of Marty's. Seymour weighed a hundred pounds more than Marty. Arlene weighed fifty pounds more than Marty. Marty did not have the strength or the physical ability to overpower either of his parents. He was, in fact, labeled "wimpy" by family and friends. "Arlene would have picked him up and thrown him through the window," said Arlene's older sister, Micky.

- Elaborating on corruption in Suffolk County: Suffolk County's most eminent forensic scientist, Ira DuBey, perjured himself many times in the courtroom while giving testimony. For openers, he lied about his credentials. Under oath, he swore he had a master's degree in forensic science; he did not. DuBey even lied about where he had gotten his undergraduate degree. He lied about prestigious courses he had taken at various schools, which he did not take. These serious allegations were brought to the attention of Suffolk County's DA's preeminent prosecutors, particularly Barry Feldman. But Feldman and others turned a blind eye and permitted Ira DuBey to lie.

Thomas Spota was himself the subject of a state and county investigation.

- To further illustrate the corruption that went on in Suffolk County, Suffolk County prosecutor David Woycik approached police officer Theodore Adamchak, a serious cop who did his job well, having handed out a hundred summonses a month, plus generating an average of forty-five yearly arrests for DWIs. This made Adamchak, in the eyes of Woycik, the perfect cop to approach. Woycik handed Adamchak his business card and told the police officer that there was a $100 dollar incentive if he would call him and direct defendants to the law office of Sullivan & Spota. [That's Thomas Spota].

- Officer Adamchak reported the bribery incident to his superiors. The matter was handed off to the bureau chief of the DA's Special Investigation Unit, James O'Rourke; also, to Detective Sergeant Alan Rosenthal, who worked in the prosecutor's office. O'Rourke and Rosenthal failed to follow up, nor was a report ever made. O'Rourke stated that he found no wrongdoing on the part of Sullivan and Spota.

- A short time later, after leaving the DA's office, O'Rourke was made a partner in the firm of Spota, Sullivan, & O'Rourke. That same year, James O'Rourke was called by the Suffolk County Legislature to testify about the matter. O'Rourke said that he was stopped from pursuing the matter by District Attorney Patrick Henry. O'Rourke was asked about Detective Sergeant Alan Rosenthal's relationship with Thomas Spota and Gerard Sullivan. "They were homosexual lovers," he said.

- Seymour Tankleff had multiple knife wounds to the neck and chest. Police officers had shown up within minutes and ordered Marty out of the house. McCready and his partner, Norman Ryan, arrived an hour later and toured the crime scene.

- Arlene had been struck on the head several times, knife wounds to neck, nearly decapitated.
- McCready writes down what he said Marty told him about the crimes. Marty never signed the so-called confession.
- Marty attends mother's funeral in prison garb three days later. Father was still in a coma [dies four weeks later.]
- Howard Asners, one of Marty's cousins, relates how Jerry Steuerman staged his disappearance.
- Forensic testing showed that neither barbell, dumbbell, nor knife had any blood or tissue on them.
- John Collins, Suffolk County prosecuting attorney, told the jury that Marty was unhappy driving around in an *old* Lincoln town car and had limited use of the family's Boston Whaler boat. Calls Marty's classmate and car mechanic as witnesses.
- Police admitted they closed their investigation as soon as Marty *confessed*; 11:56 a.m. the morning of the murders.
- Glove-type fingerprints found on light switch. No DNA testing at the time. Blood was Arlene's type.
- Drop of blood on tissue paper found in Marty's pocket, consistent with Arlene's.
- Marty said to police, "Never touched the body."
- Robert Gottlieb points out confession not consistent with physical evidence. Seymour attacked first, then Arlene, opposite from Marty's *confession*. Details of confession false.

- Gottlieb's turn to call Marty's classmates who counter those witnesses the prosecution called referencing car and boat testimony.

- Robert Gottlieb puts Marty on the stand, June 7, 1990.

- After 9 weeks of testimony, both sides rest.

- Prosecuting attorney John Collins hangs his hat on Marty's confession.

- Norman Tankleff, Seymour Tankleff's brother: "Our faith is unshaken referencing Marty's innocence."

- Frank DeAngelo, juror, said Marty had a "calm demeanor through whole trial."

- Barry Pollack, defense attorney. "Marty did not commit these murders. It's obvious."

- At time of Marty's arrest, Suffolk County homicide is under investigation for their interrogation techniques; tout an unprecedented 95% confession rate.

- McCready was accused of perjury in previous murder trials.

- Witnesses for Jay Salpeter's investigation of Marty Tankleff's innocence begin to take shape.

- Karlen Kovac's statement given in 1991, after Marty's 1990 conviction. Joseph Creedon had told Kovac he had been involved in the Tankleff murders. Creedon is connected to Glenn Harris. In 2003, Harris is in Sing Sing prison. Confides in prison priest, Father Ronald Lenmert. At the priest's urging,

Harris gives Jay Salpeter an account of his involvement. Harris says he drove Joseph Creedon and Peter Kent to the Tankleff home, after midnight, on the night of the murders. Glenn Harris waited outside in his car. Harris believes it was to be a routine burglary. When Creedon and Kent came out, they were covered in blood.

- When that new information was presented to the district attorney's office, they were not persuaded. ADA Leonard Lato said Harris has a long history of drug abuse and psychiatric issues. "Harris has no credibility at all," he said.

- Salpeter tracks down one of the alleged murder weapons, a pipe, which Joseph Creedon wanted to dispose of that night. He had Glenn stop the car and threw the pipe onto someone's wooded property. Salpeter combs the woods where Harris said he stopped the car. Using a metal detector, Jay found a pipe, but because of years gone by, it could not be tied to the crimes.

- New witnesses subsequently came forward on their own, connecting Creedon and Kent to Steuerman. Neil Fischer, a cabinet maker who did work for Jerry Steuerman in his bagel stores, testified that in 1989, he overheard Steuerman argue and tell a man ". . . something to the effect that he, Steuerman, had already killed two people, and it wouldn't matter if he killed him." Aware at the time of rumors that Steuerman had been involved in the high-profile murders, Fischer assumed the two people referred to were Seymour and Arlene Tankleff, but he initially didn't want to get involved.

- Leonard Lubrano, a restaurant owner, testified that Detective James McCready told him he did contracting work for Steuerman long before the murders. McCready had testified that he had never met Steuerman.

- "One witness blossomed into a dozen witnesses," said defense attorney Bruce Barket, now handling the Tankleff matter, trying to secure a new trial for Marty. After three years of private investigation by Salpeter, the defense concluded that the Tankleff murder victims, Seymour and Arlene, were the victims of murder for hire and that Jerry Steuerman was behind it. Still, the Suffolk County DA's office did not believe the new testimony evidence was credible enough. They refused to reopen the investigation; i.e., ADA Leonard Lato.

- Marty's defense team takes this new evidence to a judge on May 19, 2004. Judge Stephen Braslow agrees to evaluate the new information. A hearing is held July 19, 2004. Glenn Harris had given a sworn statement. Now he refuses to follow through.

- Another witness, Brian Scott Glass, said he could link Jerry Steuerman to the crime. But once he took the stand, he refused to implicate Steuerman. Glass had been pressured by authorities to change his story. Thomas Spota was the district attorney. Bruce Barket said Glass was threatened with lifetime imprisonment for a robbery charge he had pending. Marty's new defense team accused the DA's office of interfering with witnesses: "Harris, Glass, and others that we called," Barket said.

- On Feb. 4, 2005, the hearing came to an end.

- Case is argued in the media. ADA Lato labels the witnesses as "misfits," among them a nun and priest.

- Sister Angeline Matera, the nun working at Sing Sing prison, related to the Tankleff team that, "Glenn Harris spoke to me," admitting in sum and substance what Harris had told Father Ronald Lenmont.

- Judge Braslow will not grant Marty a new trial, despite all the new witnesses.
- In 2004, Joseph J. Guarascio, son of Joseph Creedon, said his father told him he killed the Tankleffs back in 1988. Steuerman gave the signal to enter the house. Glenn Harris was the getaway driver.
- Joseph Creedon's son is the fifth witness to say Creedon was involved in the murders.
- Marty wanted to take but never took a polygraph.
- No cuts or bruises on Marty, or his blood or hair found on parents, except for the swelling around his eyes, confirmed as a nose job (rhinoplasty) he received for his 17th birthday.
- "Marty's '*confessio*n' is actually evidence of his innocence," says Dr. Richard Ofshe, expert in interrogation tactics. Seymour's blood is mixed with Arlene's; her blood is not on Seymour. Indication is that Seymour was killed first. But Marty's so-called *confession* has it the other way around, saying that he first killed his mother. Many aspects of Marty's *confession* do not fit the facts.
- Back to Glenn Harris testimony: Glenn said he later watched Peter Kent burning his clothes.
- Harris takes and passes polygraph re Jay Salpeter.
- Creedon well-acquainted with Jerry's son, Todd Steuerman, a convicted drug dealer.
- Jerry Steuerman now lives in Boca Raton, Florida.

- Karlene Kovacs met Joe Creedon at a party and told her about the murders.

- Marty's team has Glenn Harris' sworn statement.

- Other witnesses come forward stating that Joe Creedon tried to involve them in the murder plot: Joe Graydon, who earlier made a failed attempt with Creedon to ambush Seymour Tankleff.

- Bill Rom, associate of Creedon, confirms Glenn Harris' story that the killers started out from his house on the night of the murders.

- Money is in it for Rom, but Rom declined. Harris did not.

- Jay Salpeter says that District Attorney Thomas Spota is doing everything to suppress the truth from coming out.

- New York State appeals court will review Judge Braslow's decision referencing all the new evidence.

- After 17 years of incarceration, Marty Tankleff was released from prison on December 27, 2007. An appellate court overturned his conviction in 2008.

- District Attorney Thomas Spota served 15 years in office before his fall.

- Joe Creedon allegedly used a bicycle brake line stripped of its plastic and bludgeoned Seymour Tankleff with it along with a gun. Peter Kent stabbed Arlene Tankleff with a knife said Joseph Guarascio, son of Joe Creedon.

- Jerry Steuerman is 85 years of age. He nor his purported accomplices/co-conspirators Joe Creedon, Peter Kent, and Glenn Harris (driver) were ever charged in the murders of Seymour and Arlene Tankleff.

- Joe Creedon is dead.

- Detective James McCready is dead.

We've now taken a good look at two high-profile cases involving Thomas Spota as a young prosecutor and Jimmy Burke as his star witness in the 1979 Johnny Pius murder matter. We've taken another sound look at Spota's involvement as district attorney in the Marty Tankleff case. In both instances, the lives of five later-declared-innocent teenagers were ruined: Michael Quartararo, Peter Quartararo, Robert Brensic, and Thomas Ryan referencing the Johnny Pius murder trials; Martin Tankleff re his parents' murders.

In Book Two, we'll examine how Thomas Spota, Jimmy Burke, and Christopher McPartland destroyed the lives of many more individuals, inclusive of intentionally thwarting the investigation of then serial killer suspect Rex Andrew Heuermann. We'll cover the Gilgo Four as well as the other Gilgo Beach/Oak Beach/Manorville victims, several prolific serial killers, genetic genealogy, and the newly-formed Gilgo Beach Homicide Investigation Task Force—inclusive of the arrest of Rex Heuermann for first- and second-degree murders of Megan Waterman, Melissa Barthelemy, and Amber Lynn Costello. Heuermann is also the Task Force's prime suspect in the murder of Maureen Brainard-Barnes. For now, let's finish up Book One by focusing on the career history of Thomas Spota and Jimmy Burke for future reference. They are now close to destroying their own lives as well.

CHAPTER TEN

Thomas J. Spota's Career History:

Thomas Spota III, born 1941, served as Suffolk County District Attorney from 2002 to 2017.

- 1971–1982: Serves as an **assistant district attorney** for Suffolk County. Includes stint as chief of homicide bureau, where he prosecuted high-profile cases, including the murder of 13-year-old John Pius of Smithtown. The case featured teenage star witness Jimmy Burke, who later became Spota's protégé.

- 1982-2001: Works in **private practice**. Gains political prominence representing county law enforcement unions.

- 2001: Switches party affiliation from Republican to Democrat to run for **district attorney** against longtime Republican DA James Catterson. After a bruising campaign, Spota wins by a large margin.

- 2003: Releases grand jury report on sexual abuse by 58 priests in the Diocese of Rockville Centre dating back decades. Wins national attention for issuing one of the first such reports in the country.

- 2005: Wins **first re-election** without an opponent and endorsed by all major and minor parties.

- 2006: Wins conviction of Islip Town Supervisor Peter McGowan, a Republican, on corruption charges stemming from illegal use of $1.2 million campaign fund.

- 2009: Wins second re-election, again without an opponent and endorsed by all major and minor parties.

- 2011: Brokers deal with County Executive Steve Levy that results in Levy not seeking a third term and turning over his $4 million campaign war chest to Spota's office. In exchange, Spota closes a criminal investigation into Levy's fundraising. Neither Spota nor Levy has ever provided a detailed explanation of the agreement.

- 2013: The state's highest court rules that Suffolk's 12-year term limit does not apply to the district attorney's office, allowing Spota to run for a fourth term. He again receives cross-endorsements from all major parties, defeats a GOP primary challenger and wins re-election.

- 2014: Secures guilty plea from Suffolk Information Technology Commissioner Donald Rodgers on misdemeanor counts related to his failing to disclose business interests on his county financial disclosure form and his work on a multimillion-dollar county software deal.

- 2014: Begins investigating then-Babylon Democratic chairman Robert Stricoff for alleged irregularities in campaign committee expenses. He later refers the case to the state Board of Elections.

- [2015: Jimmy Burke is charged by federal prosecutors with beating a man who had broken into his SUV then orchestrating a department-wide cover-up. Burke pleaded guilty and is later sentenced to 46 months in federal prison.]

- 2016: Suffolk County Executive Steve Bellone stands on the steps of Thomas Spota's office and asks for his resignation, saying Spota was heading a "criminal enterprise" that used the prosecutor's office to punish enemies and protect friends. Spota accuses Bellone of having a "personal vendetta against me for investigating and prosecuting people he is close to."

- 2016: *Newsday* reports that federal prosecutors had opened a criminal investigation into the actions of Spota's office, including handling of the Levy and Burke cases, those involving Stricoff and Rodgers, and a 2011 shooting of an unarmed cab driver by an off-duty Nassau police officer who had been drinking heavily and was never charged. Spota has denied any wrongdoing.

- May 12, 2017: Spota announces he will not seek reelection.

- 2019: Spota is convicted of obstruction, witness tampering, and conspiracy charges.

- 2020: Spota is disbarred from practicing law.

- 2021: Spota is sentenced to five years in federal prison and fined $100,000. Sentenced at the same time, Christopher McPartland received five years for his role in the corruption.

Jimmy Burke's Career History:

Jimmy Burke, born Oct. 6, 1964.

- 16 years old (going on 17) when he prepared to testified as the star witness for Thomas Spota at trial referencing the Johnny Pius' murder case.

- 20 years old on July 2, 1985 NYPD ~ cadet.
- 22 years old when hired 1986 by SCPD ~ police officer.
- 27 years old in 1991 ~ sergeant.
- 36 years old in 2000 ~ lieutenant.
- 38 years old in 2002 ~ assigned to DA's police detective squad.
- 40 years old in 2004 ~ overseeing police detectives and DA's investigators through December 2011.
- 47 years old January 2012 ~ appointed chief of police, chief of department, Suffolk County; top cop commanding 2,500 officers.
- 51 years old ~ arrested in December 2015 referencing Christopher Loeb beating.
- 52 years old ~ sentenced to 46 months plus 3 years probation on November 2, 2016.
- 54 years old ~ released from federal prison on November 23, 2018 and sent to halfway house same day; remanded to house arrest with liberal privileges: banking, shopping, et cetera.
- 54 years old James Burke officially released from federal custody on April 11, 2019. So, in essence, Burke spent 24 months in federal confinement, not 46 months.
- 59 years old in October 2023.

BOOK TWO

CHAPTER ELEVEN

Genetic genealogy will be the undoing of serial killers and other murderers. Forensic scientists take DNA samples of the unidentified victims' remains to conduct genetic genealogy testing to determine biological relationships among those individuals.

Case in point: The serial murderer referred to as the Golden State Killer, Joseph James DeAngelo—a retired California cop—was identified and apprehended through the scientific technique of genetic genealogy. In short, the police traced the killer through his family tree; that is, familial DNA searches. It did not matter that DeAngelo's DNA was not in any database because a distant relative of his was. The suspect pool was eventually narrowed down to a single family, then finally down to a single person: Joseph James DeAngelo. And the book was closed on another cold case file.

Joseph James DeAngelo

THE MANORVILLE MURDERS

Valerie Mack

Jane Doe #6 was later identified as Valerie Mack. Her partially dismembered torso was found on November 19, 2000 in a wooded area *near* Halsey Manor Road, Manorville. Eleven years later, on April 4, 2011, her head, hands, and right foot were found in a plastic bag in the vicinity of Ocean Parkway on Gilgo Beach, 47 miles away.

Jessica Taylor

Jane Doe #5 was later identified as Jessica Taylor. Her torso was discovered 2½ years later, on July 27, 2003, *off* Halsey Manor Road in Manorville. Jessica Taylor was reported missing in 2003. Her skull was found on March 29, 2011 in the Gilgo Beach area, 47 miles away from the Manorville area.

To get a detailed idea of how genetic genealogy works, let's first look into Valerie Mack's background.

Valerie was born on June 2, 1976, adopted at age 9 in 1985. Prior to that, she was shifted among seven foster homes. Valerie's sisters are Danielle Wade, and a second sister Angela. Valerie was raised in South Jersey near Atlantic City, close to marshland in the New Jersey Pine Barrens. She was involved in youth plays in Egg Harbor.

Valeries's life unraveled in 9th grade at age 14. She ran around with the wrong crowd, did drugs, skipped school, became pregnant, and left her kid with the father. Valerie bounced between Philadelphia, Pennsylvania, and New Jersey. She was arrested in Philadelphia for prostitution three times, also for drugs and loitering. Valerie returned home after an illness, and worked at a Dollar Tree store in Egg Harbor Township, New Jersey. Later, she left for New York with a guy. In 2000, her parents tried to file a missing person report with the New Jersey police. The report was never taken.

Valerie Mack's profile was uploaded into public databases. Authorities made a connection to Valerie's cousin in Georgia. That was the first step of how the FBI eventually learned Valerie's identity. A male cousin from Georgia had received a commercial DNA testing kit as a gift, allowing him to submit a DNA sample to trace his family members. A DNA match led to a living relative, an aunt, of both Valerie and the cousin; Aunt Ellen Munnings of South New Jersey.

Authorities wanted to know if Aunt Munnings had any relatives with a daughter. She could account for most of her nieces but not all the daughters of her sister, Patricia Fulton, who had been dead for almost 18 years. Patricia Fulton was the biological mother of the adopted Valerie Mack. Bingo! That is how the feds finally learned the identity of their Jane Doe, Valerie Mack. Patricia Fulton had four other children before giving birth to Valerie Lynn Fulton. All five of her children were placed in foster care.

Police then interviewed another daughter of Patricia Fulton, Tricia Hazen. DNA testing affirmed she shared the same biological mother as Valerie; i.e., Tricia and Valerie were half-sisters. Further genetic testing referencing Valerie's son, Benjamin, confirmed he was, indeed, Valerie's son.

JOHN BITTROLFF

LET'S GO BACK IN TIME: 1993 – 2014

When discussing the Manorville murders of Valerie Mack and Jessica Taylor, we need to take a close look at John Bittrolff.

John Bittrolff was born July 1, 1966. He was age 48 when arrested in 2014 and convicted in 2017 for the murders of two women: Rita Tangredi, and Colleen McNamee.

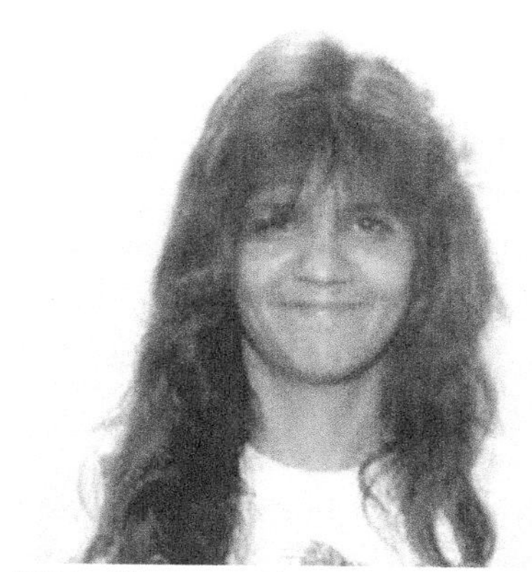

Rita Tangredi

ColleenMcNamee

The nude body of 31-year-old sex worker Rita Tangredi of East Patchogue was discovered in a wooded area in East Patchogue on

November 2, 1993. The killer had bludgeoned Rita and strangled her to death.

Three months later, on January 30, 1994, the naked remains of 20-year-old Colleen McNamee of Holbrook were discovered in a forested area near the William Floyd Parkway in Shirley. Like Rita, Colleen had been beaten and strangled to death. Woodchips were found on both bodies.

Bittrolff was a possible suspect in a third murder, that of Sandra Costilla. Costilla's body was discovered on November 21, 1993 in North Sea Southampton, near Fish Cove.

Sandra Costilla

John Bittrolff lived at 167 Silas Carter Road in Manorville, with his wife and two sons from 1997 to 2014 when he was arrested for the two murders. Neighbors were shocked. He was always helpful and pleasant. Like so many serial killers, you would never know. He was a carpenter and self-employed: Coastline Construction was the name of his company.

Rita Tangredi and Colleen McNamee were both sex workers who were killed in a similar fashion. Their bodies were found nude and posed, one arm above the head. Colleen and Rita were both missing a single shoe or sneaker.

For more than 20 years, their murders had remained unsolved. However, in 2013, John Bittrolff's brother, Timothy, was arrested for an unrelated crime. As a result, he was forced to submit to a DNA sample. Not long afterwards, Timothy's sample proved to be a familial match with the DNA evidence that had been collected from the bodies of Rita Tangredi and Colleen McNamee: semen.

The DNA match proved that Timothy was closely related to the likely killer of Tangredi and McNamee. As a result, John Bittrolff quickly became the prime suspect in the two murders. At that stage, investigators started using a bogus plumber's van to keep Bittrolff under surveillance. Their goal was to follow the carpenter until he discarded an item with his DNA on it. However, Bittrolff immediately saw through this facąde and realized that he was being tailed by the police. At one point, he even pulled an evasive driving maneuver in an attempt to lose them.

Detectives noted that John Bittrolff had a lot of beer bottles at home. However, he never put any of these bottles into the household recycling bin. Furthermore, when the lab tested other items from the family's garbage, they were only able to find samples belonging to his wife and two sons. All of this suggested that Bittrolff had a basic knowledge of forensic science and that he knew why he was a suspect.

After failing to find a DNA sample of John's in the household garbage, the police eventually decided to pull John Bittrolff over and bring him in for questioning. During questioning, he drank from a cup that they offered him. This cup gave investigators a sample of his DNA, which proved to be a perfect match with the evidence that had been found on both Tangredi and McNamee.

Was John Bittrolff active during the time of other murders?

Sandra Costilla, body discovered 1993, Bittrolff age 27, suspected of her murder.

Rita Tangredi, body discovered 1993, Bittrolff age 27, accused and convicted of her murder.

Colleen McNamee, body discovered 1994, Bittrolff age 28, accused and convicted of her murder.

Valerie Mack disappeared in 2000. Her torso was found November 2000 in Manorville. Her head, hands, and right foot were found near Gilgo Beach in 2011, 47 miles away. Bittrolff age 34.

Jessica Taylor disappeared in 2003. Her torso was found on July 2003 in Manorville. Her skull was found in Gilgo Beach in 2011, Bittrolff age 37.

The Gilgo Four:

Maureen Brainard-Barnes disappeared 2007. Bittrolff age 41.

Melissa Barthelemy disappeared 2009. Bittrolff age 43.

Megan Waterman disappeared June 2010. Bittrolff age 44.

Amber Lynn Costello disappeared September 2010. Bittrolff still age 44.

Reminder: Shannan Gilbert disappeared May 1, 2010. Bittrolff age 44. Point being, John Bittrolff was around at the time to have killed *some* of the LISK victims.

Virtually all the victims were female, petite (between 4 feet 10 inches and 5 feet 5 inches tall), attractive. They were beaten and/or strangled; some of the bodies were posed. But Bittrolff is not considered a suspect in the LISK murders say the police. Why? Because the perp's M.O. (Modus Operandi, i.e., method of operating) is different some law enforcement officials maintain. REALLY? Is that the real reason**?**

Factoid: Serial Killers can and do change their M.O., and the police, of course, know that fact. John Bittrolff was certainly savvy enough to have changed his M.O. When a person or group of bad actors do not want you looking over *here*, they divert your attention over *there*.

As a reminder, in 1993 and 1994, police found the remains of two women's torsos in Manorville. Those Jane Doe's were identified as Valerie Mack and Jessica Taylor. More than 20 years later, a good many folks speculate that John Bittrolff may have been connected to two of the Gilgo Beach murders, and with good reason: The torso of the first victim found in Manorville, 21 years earlier, belonged to Valerie Mack. On November 19, 2000, three pheasant hunters discovered the torso in a wooded area near Halsey Manor Road, Manorville. Their dog found the remains wrapped in layers of garbage bags after going into a thicket. In 2011, the skull, hands, and right foot of same woman was found in proximity to Gilgo Beach, 47 miles away. She was later identified as Valerie Mack ~ Jane Doe #6. Two and a half years later, the torso of a second victim was found in Manorville in 2003. Also in 2011, the skull of that same woman was found in proximity to Gilgo Beach, later identified as Jessica Taylor ~ Jane Doe #5. The two dump sites in Manorville were half a mile apart. The distance between East Patchogue and Manorville is 13 miles; that is, 20 minutes by car referencing Rita Tangredi; age 20. North Shirley and Manorville are 8.6 miles apart; that is, 12 minutes by car referencing Colleen McNamee; age 31. Gilgo Beach and Manorville are 45.7 miles apart; that is, 47 minutes by car referencing Valerie Mack. North Sea Southampton and Manorville are 24.7 miles apart; that is, 29 minutes by car referencing Sandra Costilla. John Bittrolff was *suspected* of her murder in 1993.

John Bittrolff may be connected to Melissa Barthelemy. In September of 2017, the mother of Melissa Barthelemy stated that her daughter had made many cellphone calls to Manorville.

In 2011, the police uncovered Jessica Taylor and Valerie Mack's partial remains found along Ocean Parkway, Gilgo Beach—close to where the killer disposed of the bodies of the Gilgo Four. This discovery shows the likelihood that John Bittrolff could be one of the serial killers and that he was possibly working in concert with another murderer—or others.

Following Bittrolff's conviction for the murders of Rita Tangredi and Colleen McNamee, the Suffolk County district attorney publicly announced that he was a prime suspect in the LISK case. Interestingly, the focus has shifted to other suspects such as James Burke, Peter Hackett, Joseph Brewer, Michael Pak, even James Bissett.

After an anonymous phone call to police, Rita Tangredi was found murdered, her body located off Esplanade Drive in East

Patchogue on November 2, 1993. The body of Colleen McNamee was found almost three months later, close to Express Drive South, near William Floyd Parkway in Shirley on January 30, 1994. Both victims had been badly beaten and their bodies similarly posed; one arm raised, one shoe/sneaker missing. Woodchips were found on both bodies.

Attorney William Keahon with Defendant John Bittrolff

The prosecution based its case on science and the use of DNA in its infancy. John Bittrolff's semen had been collected from the Manorville's victims' bodies. Attorney William (Billy) Keahon based Bittrolff's defense case on the accusation of corruption; that is, the destroying of evidence that would have initially and likely implicated two police officers in the murder of Colleen McNamee and Rita Tangredi.

Suffolk County Police Sergeant Michael Murphy of the Fifth Precinct had been a suspect since 1998, along with another police officer, Teddy Hart, in the double murder of Colleen McNamee of Holbrook, and Rita Tangredi of East Patchogue. Wood shavings had been found in Sergeant Murphy's police vehicle.

Sgt. Michael Murphy

Referencing the crime scene photos, no photographs of the woodchips were in any of the crime scene photos, nor the wood shavings taken from suspect Sergeant Michael Murphy's police vehicle—as they should have been. The evidence had been destroyed! Officer Teddy Hart was later fired for making threats of violence toward women. Sergeant Michael Murphy, whose father was Thomas Murphy, the department's chief of detectives at the time, was promoted to lieutenant. Sound familiar?

The Suffolk County Police Department destroyed the evidence in both those murder cases. The department also destroyed evidence that might have linked its sergeant to both murders. The excuse for its destruction was that the evidence had not been properly identified as homicide evidence. This was testified to by Officer Linda Passarella, a 13-year veteran of the department's property bureau, during the murder trial of John Bittrolff.

FACTS REFERENCING JOHN BITTROLFF'S ARREST:

- Michael Murphy had been accused of frequenting prostitutes at the Patchogue Motor Inn, Patchogue.

- Michael Murphy impregnated a 15-year-old girl and purportedly made her leave the country.

- DNA evidence was a falsified court document. A female employee, unnamed, was suspended and then retired. First case of familial (genetic genealogy) DNA testing in the state of New York.

- The former director of forensic science at the New York Department of Criminal Justice Services (DCJS) stated that the Office of Forensic Science (OFS) made three catastrophic DNA identification errors and falsified a fourth certification document. The claims were made by Brian Gestring, a member of the state's Commission on Forensic Science. He said the errors exposed a "huge problem" with the forensic science work being done for the Department of Criminal Justice Services.

- Gestring said that the falsified certification document involved the investigation of John Bittrolff, imprisoned for the murder of the two prostitutes, referring to Rita Tangredi and Colleen McNamee.

- Mr. Keahon, John Bittrolff's defense attorney, stated that the Suffolk police destroyed a total of 148 pieces of evidence concerning the murder of Colleen McNamee in 2007.

- Mr. Biancavilla, the prosecutor, acknowledged that fact, but added that the evidence was "mistakenly destroyed." "We're not perfect," he said, calling the mistake "a speed bump or hiccup along the way."

- Mr. Keahon told the jury, "I'm unable to see that evidence now and have it analyzed. It's gone! Destroyed. And the prosecutor refers to that as a bump in the road."

- Retired Suffolk County Detective John McLear testified in New York State Supreme Court that Michael Murphy was a suspect in the murders. The case went dormant from 2006 to 2012. Evidence collected from both crime scenes and Murphy's police vehicle had been destroyed. **Note:** You do not destroy evidence in a murder investigation—Ever! Period.

- A woman testified in court that Michael Murphy had her perform "free oral sex some seven or eight times over the course of two years."

- The DNA link to John Bittrolff and his arrest came in 2014. Former Detective William Rathjen testified: "Rita Tangredi's body was the first to be discovered." As he trapsed through the area, he found a blue winter jacket, socks, one sneaker, stretch pants, and black jeans. And then he found Tangredi.

- Colleen McNamee was the second victim to be found three months later. Both bodies were posed: naked, legs spread, one arm raised overhead. Both victims' skulls had been crushed. McNamee's fingerprints were on file; hence, available identification.

- Rita Tangredi, 31 years old of East Patchogue, was found on November 2, 1993.

- Colleen McNamee, 20 years old of Holbrook was found January 30, 1994.

- The Manorville murders stopped in 1994. The Long Island Serial Killer crimes started in 1996.

- John Bittrolff was charged with the two murders in July 2014, arraigned on July 31, 2014. On July 5, 2017, John Bittrolff was convicted of the murders.

- May 2022. Attorney John Ray asks for Suffolk County Police Lieutenant Kevin Beyrer's resignation. John Ray wants Beyrer out of the picture because of his close ties to the Oak Beach community. "Beyrer is the only holdout from the James Burke days" said Ray, attorney for the Shannan Gilbert and Jessica Taylor families. Ray hopes that our new Suffolk County Police Commissioner Rodney Harrison will pursue the truth re Shannan Gilbert's death.

CHAPTER TWELVE

Suffolk County Police Commissioner Rodney K. Harrison, a 30-year veteran with the City of New York Police Department, left that position as chief of department to become Suffolk County's new police commissioner. Harrison was confirmed on December 23, 2021, and sworn into office on January 11, 2022.

Suffolk County Police Commissioner Rodney Harrison

Harrison learned early on that only one homicide detective was assigned to the Gilgo case. Not only that, but the detective was juggling other assignments as well. "This case is never gonna be solved like that," snapped Harrison, "especially if this person, this detective, is also catching other cases." Harrison increased the number of detectives to four. "We're going to take these individuals and put them in a place where they're only looking at Gilgo," he concluded.

On February 15, 2022, Harrison announced the creation of a special joint task force, comprised of investigators from the Suffolk

County Police Department, District Attorney's office, Suffolk County Sheriff's office, New York State Police, and the FBI. The team is titled The Gilgo Beach Homicide Investigation Task Force, inclusive of local, state, and federal agencies all working together.

Raymond A. Tierney, a prosecutor for more than 27 years at both state and federal levels, was elected as Suffolk County's new district attorney on November 2, 2021. He assumed office on January 1, 2022.

There is a $50,000 reward leading to the arrest and conviction of the Long Island Serial Killer(s), raised from $25,000.

REX ANDREW HEUERMANN'S JULY 13, 2023 ARREST AS A SUSPECT IN THE LONG ISLAND SERIAL KILLER MURDERS

District Attorney Ray Tierney addressed the media and announced the arrest of a 60-year-old Nassau County man from Massapequa Park, Long Island, New York. Rex Andrew Heuermann is a Manhattan-based architect charged on Friday, July 14, 2023 with three counts each of first- and second-degree murder in the deaths of Melissa Barthelemy, Megan Waterman, and Amber Lynn Costello. Additionally, Heuermann is the prime suspect in the murder of Maureen Brainard-Barnes, the fourth victim relating to the Gilgo Four. Their bodies were found by police in December of 2010 near a wooded area of Gilgo Beach along Ocean Parkway.

Rex Heuermann

DNA evidence was recovered from pizza crust and a used napkin that Heuermann had discarded outside his Manhattan office, linking him to three of the victims. Moreover, authorities connected his whereabouts to cellular phone site data at key times and locations. Heuermann was arrested without incident near his office on Thursday, July 13, 2023. As mentioned, the task force had decided to pull the plug early on regarding the investigation over concerns that the situation was becoming more dangerous. Heuermann was still using the services of sex workers and might strike again and/or flee authorities believed.

Heuermann also owns property in Chester, South Carolina as well as a time-share in Las Vegas, Nevada. He used seven burner phones over the course of a 14-month period to search some 200-plus times information referencing the Gilgo Beach investigation. That seventh burner phone was recovered at the time of the suspect's arrest.

Through several calls using Melissa Barthelemy cellphone number to call and torment her 15-year-old sister, Amanda, a man spoke in a calm voice. "Do you know what your sister is?" he questioned. "She's a whore. Do you think you'll ever speak to her again?" There were several other calls made to Amanda.

Tierney states that Heuermann's Internet searches were not only limited to photos of the victims. "There were pictures of the victims' relatives, their sisters, their children. He was trying to locate those individuals. In addition to that, there was a lot of torture porn and what you would consider depictions of women being abused, being raped, and being killed." Heuermann also searched for child porn.

At a news conference that Friday afternoon, Suffolk County Police Commissioner Rodney Harrison said, "Rex Heuermann is a demon that walks among us." District Attorney Ray Tierney personally handled the arraignment and will also try the case in court. Evidence included the impoundment of two first-generation Chevrolet Avalanche pickup trucks. One green model (bought in 2002) was initially owned and driven by Rex Heuermann at the time of the murders (2010) and later signed over to his brother, Craig Heuermann (2012). It is this vehicle that authorities say was seen by a witness in

2010, parked in the driveway at the home of Amber Lynn Costello, 1112 America Avenue in West Baylon, as well as the following night on September 2, 2010, when she was last seen. Rex Heuermann had subsequently purchased a later model Avalanche, which was removed from his home in Massapequa Park on July 14, 2023. An *avalanche* of evidence, pun intended, has been collected to support the charges brought against Heuermann. Voluminous pages of damning information (8 terabytes and 100 hours of surveillance video footage outside his home and Manhattan office it was reported) were turned over, and continues to be turned over to the defense "on a rolling basis," said District Attorney Tierney.

It was the vehicle information that helped crack the case when the witness was reinvestigated by detectives of the Gilgo Beach Homicide Investigation Task Force. Rex Heuermann was identified as a prime suspect by the team on March 14, 2022 and had been under *vigilant* surveillance from that moment until his arrest on July 13, 2023. District Attorney Tierney stated at a news conference that for each of the four murders, "Heuermann got an individual burner phone, and he used that to communicate with the victims; and then shortly after the death of the victims, he would get rid of the burner phone."

Outside the courthouse following Rex Heuermann's arraignment, defense attorney, Michael J. Brown of Central Islip had said that the case against his client is "extremely circumstantial in nature. I can tell you what he did say as he was in tears. 'I didn't do this,'" the attorney added. "Everyone is presumed innocent in our country."

Michael Brown, Attorney for Rex Heuermann

District Attorney Ray Tierney spoke about Heuermann's online activity, which included "thousands of searches related to sex workers, sadistic torture-related pornography, and child pornography," he stated. "I think when you look at his Internet searches, that provides a little insight into his state of mind," Tierney continued.

Heuermann is married with two children, one of whom works with him (his daughter Victoria) at the Chelsea area architectural firm in Midtown Manhattan, located at 385 Fifth Avenue and the corner of 35th Street. The couple also has a special needs son. Heuermann's wife, Asa Ellerup, married 27 years, refused to comment at her husband's arraignment just outside the courtroom when approached by a reporter. "Please leave me alone," she stated firmly. "I will not be saying anything," apparently still in a state of shock when first learning of the charges brought against her husband. After digesting the facts explained to her by Police Commissioner Rodney Harrison, Ellerup flatly stated, "Okay, it is what it is." She filed for divorce several days after absorbing the news that her husband led a double life.

From left to right: Asa Ellerup, daughter Victoria, Son Christoper Sheridan

Neighbors had a mix of both positive and negative comments referencing the couple and their suburban home at 105 First Avenue in Massapequa Park, near the corner of Michigan Avenue. Namely, the family's unkempt appearance of that residence, juxtaposed among the well-manicured landscaped lawns along the block, especially noted by those who knew the man to be a Manhattan architect—not to mention the weathered red shingles and thin wooden support beams that held up the front porch. The Heuermann home is less than a 20-mile drive from Gilgo Beach, a direct route down the Wantagh Parkway, onto Ocean Parkway.

The Heuermann Home

Longtime resident Cheryl Lombardi said, "It's a little scary. Every time we walked past, we asked, 'Why didn't they fix this house up?' It's the only one in the neighborhood that looks like this."

Neighbors would see him walking to the Massapequa Park Train Station, en route to Manhattan, wearing big oval eyeglasses, business suit, vest, tie, and briefcase in hand.

Rex Heuermann in Manhattan

Etienne Devillers, a retired New York City firefighter who lives next door to Heuermann, said, "He's been a quiet guy. We just say hello in the mornings . . . and afternoon pleasantries. Nothing special. We never associated in any way."

Ironically, Michael McManus, a Massapequa Park resident who lives nearby, hosts a Gilgo Beach podcast and has closely followed the case over the last decade. He credited Police Commissioner Harrison and the team for maintaining continued pressure in the investigation, adding, "But the fact that it's in this exact town is kind of alarming."

Massapequa Park resident Richard Harmon echoes the sentiment of Michael McManus. "It's a shocker! It's a real eye-opener," said Harmon. "Living here for 29 years, this is the worst case I've ever seen. Nobody suspected this."

Actor Billy Baldwin was Rex Heuermann's fellow high school classmate in 1981. "Woke up this morning to learn that the Gilgo

Beach serial killer suspect was my high school classmate." Berner High School, Massapequa, graduating class of 1981. "Average guy... quiet, family man. Mind-boggling . . . Massapequa is in shock."

Fifteen years ago, next-door neighbor Dominick Cancellieri saw and smelled Heuermann digging and burning trash in his backyard during the early morning hours every few weeks.

Many a year ago, neighbors would see his father known for jogging with hatchet in hand, fighting off coyotes and neighbors' dogs.

In July of 2023, forensic personnel were seen digging a hole in the backyard of Heuermann's property with an excavator. They find small fragments on a board within the soil. At that point, they are split as to whether the pieces are bone, human or otherwise. They await lab analysis. The team is playing it close to the vest, remaining silent on their findings. Others were seen digging with spades and shovels. Within the six-room wood-paneled home, a two- to three-foot concrete basement vault had been constructed, housing more than 280 guns, comprised of rifles, shotguns, and handguns. A rope was also recovered from the vault, along with handcuff keys on a shelf underneath a workbench. Heuermann is an avid sportsman who would invite colleagues to go shooting or hunting, including deer and bear hunting trips. He'd describe in detail the process of dressing deer or baiting an area and lying in wait of a bear.

Of the cache of weapons seized from the vault, *Newsday* later reported that Suffolk County prosecutors had confiscated at least 26 unregistered handguns, 15 unregistered assault weapons, and 10 high-capacity magazines, all in violation of New York State's firearms laws.

Nichole Brass, a former escort who had dinner with the accused Gilgo Beach serial killer Rex Heuermann, said he "got off" talking about the victims and spouted specific information referencing some of the cases that was not widely known at the time.

Nicole went out with Rex Heuermann in either 2012 or 2014 to earn money to pay for her drug addiction. Heuermann blithefully spoke about the Gilgo Beach murders. "When he spoke about the murders, it was almost like he was visualizing it in his head and getting off to what he was saying," Brass related to the *New York Post*.

In another interview with *Good Morning America*, Brass said that Heuermann "had this smile on his face and a glossed-over look in his eye when talking about the Gilgo Beach murders, which left me with a really, really bad feeling. My gut was telling me I had to get away from him. At the time, I was in my early 20s, and I was an addict. I wasn't really thinking about safety," she said.

Brass reportedly said she connected with Heuermann through one of those escort sites, leading to their encounter at the Steamroom seafood restaurant in Port Jefferson.

She said Heuermann initially wanted to rent a hotel room for them, but she did not feel comfortable meeting him in private, so she convinced him to take her out to dinner instead.

"In the beginning, he seemed totally normal," Brass recalled. "He talked about his job and just seemed really normal, until he brought up the Gilgo Beach murders."

Heuermann asked Brass if she was a true-crime fan, and the two talked about several famous serial killers. "Then he said, 'Have you heard of the Gilgo Beach murders?' and that's when he got real weird," Brass explained.

Brass related that Heuermann mentioned details about the killings that she had not heard before, despite closely following the investigation.

"I was following the case, and he mentioned one of the girls I hadn't heard about yet. It seemed like he was talking about it from experience, not a point of view," she said.

Brass added that it seemed like the man did not feel at all sorry for the victims and was excited to discuss the killings. "He seemed like somebody who really wanted to brag about what they did, but couldn't."

As Heuermann spoke, Brass said, "Something about his body language changed, the look in his eyes changed, and it seemed like talking about the victims was enjoyable for him."

Brass recalled getting "the worst gut feeling about him" during their dinner date, which she rushed to finish as quickly as possible because she was "so scared," she said.

Heuermann tried to talk Brass into leaving her car in the parking lot and riding with him to the hotel room he had booked for them, but Nicole refused. "He was like, leave your car; come in mine. He was very adamant about me leaving my car. Looking back, he didn't want to have to kill somebody and get rid of their car."

Brass said she never went to the police with her suspicions about Heuermann because she was on parole for a drug conviction at the time. "I'm a felon and had a history and didn't want to get involved with cops," Brass explained. "I think he went after girls who were addicts or had a record, or anyone less likely to talk to police."

When Brass learned of Heuermann's arrest, she felt both vindicated and conflicted about not going to the cops after her dinner date. "I was also like, holy shit! I was right. Maybe I should have spoken to the cops, but I knew they wouldn't listen to me." Her chilling dinner date with Rex Heuermann left Nicole Brass fearing for her life.

Court papers say Rex Heuermann is the caller who made those taunting cellphone calls to Melissa Barthelemy's younger sister, Amanda. FBI investigators had triangulated the data from different burner phones and immediately homed in on similarities. The calls went through four cell towers in the Massapequa Park area.

"The perpetrator of those crimes," said District Attorney Ray Tierney, "was probably located in that area at or around the times of the murders." Additionally, FBI investigators traced the burner phones to a section of Manhattan, where it was later learned Rex Heuermann had his office. Furthermore, the Gilgo Beach Homicide Investigation Task Force learned that cellphone data placed Heuermann within the area around Gilgo Beach at the time when one of the victims went missing.

Digital forensics expert and cyber crime detective Tiffany Lenart states that Rex Heuermann's credit card records are damning.

"He was smart enough to use a burner phone in communication with sex workers, but he paid for it with his own American Express card."

In sum and substance, Lenart points to "layers of digital evidence: cell tower records, financial records, records from his service provider for his IP addresses from home and all call work records from his cellphone; and they're connecting when and where these phones were when these girls went missing. Heuermann takes the victims' phones, and he doesn't turn them off. He makes calls from the phones all in the same places, so there are overlapping patterns of activity where the phones are all together. He had multiple burner phones. This happens on different occasions. It's pinging in Massapequa when he's home and when he's in Manhattan. Authorities know he's in Manhattan because they're checking his financials; that is, he's using his American Express card. At the same time, the victims are checking their e-mails, calling home, and it happens that his burner phones are in the same place as the victims' cellphones. Heuermann was checking the victims' voicemails from their phones that he took."

Lenart speculates that Heuermann may have gotten a PIN code from the victims to access their voicemails, or maybe the phones allowed anyone to get access. Lenart further states, "We don't know what model of phone(s) they were. Heuermann was checking to see if anyone is looking for his victims.

"Heuermann makes mistakes when creating fake names for burner phones. He is using information that relates back to him, such as his middle name," she continues.

"All prior messages on his phone will be there unless he has manually deleted them. The authorities may be able to retrieve location data from the Chevy Avalanche(s) navigation system(s). If Heuermann connected his cellphone to the vehicle(s), messages, call logs, checking e-mail, et cetera. would be available from the navigation system in the truck(s)."

In all fairness to the earlier investigations performed by well-meaning forensic folks working with DNA analyses during the prior administrations, District Attorney Ray Tierney points out that it was "not technologically feasible around the time of the murders" to specifically home in on a suspect, which does not excuse the inept performance of law enforcement officials who botched and/or purposely moved the investigation off track.

In 2010, investigators found a single hair removed from the body of Megan Waterman. Thirteen years later, refined genetic testing revealed that the source of that single strand of hair was linked to Rex Heuermann. An example of this scientific breakthrough was made possible by the upgrading advancements referencing mitochondrial DNA.

Without getting too heavy-handed, let us take a moment to begin to understand this new, amazing, decade-plus-long development. A mitochondrial DNA team examines biological items of evidence from crime scenes to determine the mitochondrial DNA sequence from samples such as hair, bones, teeth, and skin cells collected from under fingernails. In the past, these items contained low concentrations of degraded DNA, making them unsuitable for nuclear DNA examinations. The most important advantage of utilizing advanced mitochondrial (mtDNA) testing is its intrinsic ability to resist degradation and enhance its high copy number inside the cell as compared to nuclear (nDNA) DNA.

Rex Heuermann was linked to the murder of Megan Waterman after recovering DNA from a box of discarded pizza crust along with a paper napkin from the trash container retrieved outside his office. The DNA matched a hair found at the bottom of camo-patterned burlap used to "constrain, wrap, and transport" Waterman's body.

Heuermann's wife's DNA was found on the bodies of three of the four victims, believed to be transfer material from her to him. A water bottle collected from outside the home was a match to a sample of a woman's hair found on the tape used to tie up Megan Waterman and Amber Lynn Costello, including one of three leather belts with the embossed letters WH or HM [depending on how you held the belt], used to bind Maureen Brainard-Barnes' chest area. The public first learned the name of the victim bound with one of the three belts in the late summer of 2023. If the initials are to be interpreted as WH, Rex Heuermann's grandfather was William Heuermann, who died in 1964

". . . so, assign to that what you will," said District Attorney Ray Tierney. As mentioned, Rex Heuermann has not been charged with Maureen Brainard-Barnes' murder, yet he is a prime suspect in the case.

CHAPTER THIRTEEN

TIMELINE REFERENCING GENERAL INFORMATION CELLPHONE/BURNER PHONE CALLS & PHYSICAL EVIDENCE

CELLPHONES & BURNER PHONES

Note: Asa Ellerup (Rex Heuermann's wife) was out of town, state or country during the times that the Gilgo Four murders took place, police say. Authorities maintain that Ellerup was not involved in any wrongdoing and that the physical evidence (her hairs) was the result of transference; i.e., clothing, et cetera.

Maureen Brainard-Barnes, 25 years old, working as a sex worker, lived in Norwich, Connecticut. On July 6, 2007, she traveled by Amtrak from New London, Connecticut to New York City and was last seen on July 9, 2007. Between July 6, 2007 and July 9, 2007, there were sixteen interactions between Rex Heuermann's burner phone and Brainard-Barnes' cellphone. On July 9, 2007, her phone was traced to Midtown Manhattan near the 59th Street bridge at 11:56 p.m. On July 12, two outbound calls were made on her phone off the Long Island Expressway near Islandia, New York. The calls were made by someone checking Maureen's voicemail.

Melissa Barthelemy, 24 years old, was last seen on July 10, 2009 in New York City. At the time, she was working as a sex worker. On July 3, 2009, Barthelemy was contacted by a burner phone. Thereafter, Barthelemy was contacted by burner phone on July 6, July 9, and July

10, 2009 before she was last seen in Midtown Manhattan. On July 10, 2009, cell site records showed that the burner phone traveled from Massapequa Park to Midtown Manhattan. Later that evening, the burner phone traveled from Midtown Manhattan to Massapequa, with the last cell site location being in Massapequa on July 11, 2009 at 1:43 a.m. On July 11, 2009, Barthelemy's cellphone was used to make an outbound call, checking her voicemail from a cell site location in Freeport, Long Island. On July 11 and July 12, 2009, Barthelemy's phone was used to check her voicemail from a Babylon location. On July 17, July 23, August 5, and August 26, 2009, Barthelemy's cellphone was used by a male to make taunting calls from Midtown Manhattan to Barthelemy's family, specifically Melissa's sister Amanda, saying that he had raped and killed Melissa. Barthelemy was the first victim found in 2010; the second victim killed after Maureen Brainard-Barnes.

On July 10, 2009, Heuermann's wife, Asa Ellerup, traveled to Iceland. On August 18, 2009, Heuermann's wife returned to the United States.

Megan Waterman, 22 years old, was working as a sex worker. Waterman was the third victim of the Gilgo Four. She lived in Scarborough, Maine. Waterman headed to New York City with her pimp and stayed at several hotels and motels on Long Island, including the Extended Stay America in Bethpage. Waterman was last seen alive leaving the Holiday Inn Express Hotel in Hauppauge on June 6, 2010, at approximately 1:30 a.m. She told her pimp (who was in Brooklyn at the time) that she was going to a convenience store near the hotel. On June 5, 2010, Waterman's cellphone was contacted by a newly activated burner phone, according to court records. Waterman communicated with the burner phone up until June 6, 2010 at 1:31 a.m. when surveillance video showed her leaving the Holiday Inn. Waterman's cellphone was traced back to Massapequa Park at approximately 3:11 a.m., which is in the vicinity of Rex Heuermann's home.

On June 4, 2010, Heiermann's wife travels to Maryland. On June 8, Heuermann's wife returns to New York from Maryland.

Amber Lynn Costello, 27 years old, was last seen on September 2, 2010, leaving her home in West Babylon. At the time, she was working as a sex worker. She had tattoos on her neck, a butterfly on her lower back, and the name Margaret on a leg. She lived with a woman and two men who were all drug addicts. Costello advertised her services on Craigslist and Backpage to support the four's drug habit. Costello's aliases were Carolina or Mia. Costello had moved to New York from Clearwater, Florida. She spent 28 days in a rehab program, then relapsed. Costello was not reported missing. Her body was found by police December 13, 2010 on the north side of Ocean Parkway.

Costello and her roommates would sometimes scam her clients, whereby the client pays money up front and her male roommate would suddenly show up feigning outrage and say that Amber was his girlfriend. The client would then take off.

On September 1, 2010, Costello was contacted by burner phone at 11:33 p.m. and 11:34 p.m. from cell site locations in West Amityville and Massapequa Park. From there, the burner phone traveled to West Babylon in proximity to Costello's residence and had contact with Costello's cellphone at 12:05 a.m. on September 2, 2010.

According to witnesses, around the time of these communications between the burner phone and Costello's cellphone, a client arrived at Costello's home. A witness described seeing a dark pickup truck parked in front of Costello's home in West Babylon. After the client entered the home, a ruse, as described above, began. The client, who, not wanting an altercation, walked out, leaving his $1,500 behind on a table. The witness reported that the client had said he was just a friend and to tell her, "I'll give her a call later," as he walked out the door. Based on subsequent interviews, the client was described as a large white male, approximately 6'4"–6'6", in his mid-forties, approximately 240 pounds, dark bushy hair, and wearing big oval-style 1970s eyeglasses.

One witness said that the client drove a first-generation Chevy Avalanche, which had been parked in the driveway. Around 1:18 a.m.,

Costello received a text message from the burner phone which said, "That was not nice, so do I get credit for next time?" Phone records show a text message was later sent from the cellphone two minutes away from Massapequa Park. According to a witness, Costello was contacted by the same client later that day. A witness said, "Amber told us that he wanted to see her again, but he didn't want to come back to the house because of her boyfriend." Costello had been contacted by cellphone four times that night between 9:30 p.m. and 11:17 p.m. with calls being traced back to Midtown Manhattan, then Massapequa Park, then West Babylon. Costello was last seen leaving her home in West Babylon on September 2, 2010. She left her cellphone behind. Shortly after Costello left the house, one of the witnesses saw a dark-colored truck pass the house, coming from the direction Costello had walked towards.

On August 28, 2010, Heuermann's wife traveled to New Jersey. On September 5, 2010, Heuermann's wife, Asa Ellerup, returned home to New York from New Jersey.

Records obtained from the Suffolk County District Attorney's Office revealed that the burner phone consistently had activity on the cellular towers that provided coverage to Rex Heuermann's residence in Massapequa Park and his business in New York City. Legal process served on Google seeking records or accounts associated with the device identifiers of these additional burner phones revealed a connection to yet another "burner" or "junk" e-mail account, namely thawk080672@gmail.com (hereinafter the "Thawk E-mail Account"). Google records further indicated that the Thawk E-mail Account was subscribed in the fictitious name "Thomas Hawk." A search warrant revealed that the Thawk E-mail Account, associated with burner phone 347-304-2671, was used to conduct thousands of searches related to sex workers, sadistic torture-related pornography, and child pornography, including:

1. mistress long island
2. mature escorts Manhattan

3. girl begging for rape porn
4. teen girl begging for rape porn
5. pretty girl with bruised face porn
6. torture redhead porn
7. 10-year-old school girl
8. henta[i] plump pussy lips cut off porn
9. skinny red head tied up porn
10. short fat girl tied up po[r]n
11. tied up and raped porn
12. Asian twink [a gay or effeminate male regarded as an object of homosexual desire] tied up porn
13. tied slave force fed cock
14. cum shot and crying porn
15. girl hog tied torture porn
16. 10-year-old blonde hair girl
17. Chubby 10-year-old girl
18. Black girl 10 years old
19. Girl with face beat up
20. Chubby 10-year-old girl crying
21. 13-year-old school girl
22. Age 12 child girl with blonde hair and blue eyes
23. Blonde hair girl young depressed
24. Teen girl oiled bodies
25. Preteen girl with makeup
26. Nude slave girls
27. Old Janitors gangbang little school girl
28. Crying girl painful anal
29. School girl
30. Crying teen porn

The Thawk E-mail Account was also used to conduct more than two hundred (200) searches between March 2022 and June 2023, related to active and known serial killers, the specific disappearances and murders of Maureen Brainard-Barnes, Melissa Barthelemy, Megan Waterman, and Amber Costello, and the investigation into their murders. These searches or articles include, but are not limited to:

1. "why could law enforcement not trace the calls made by the long island serial killer"
2. "why hasn't the long island serial killer been caught"
3. "Long Island killer"
4. "Long Island Serial Killer Phone Call"
5. "Long Island Serial Killer update"
6. "Long Island Serial Killer Update 2022"
7. "FBI active serial killers"
8. "Serial Killers by State 2023"
9. "Map of all known serial killers"
10. "unsolved serial killer cases"
11. "America's 5 most notorious old cases"
12. "11 Currently Active Serial Killers"
13. "8 Terrifying Active Serial Killers (We Can't Find)"
14. "John Bittrolff"
15. "Megan Waterman"
16. "Melissa Barthelemy"
17. "Maureen Brainard-Barnes"
18. "[Redacted – name of relative of Melissa] Barthelemy"
19. "[Redacted – name of relative of Megan] Waterman"
20. "Cops launch Gilgo Beach Homicide Investigation Task Force"
21. "Mapping the Long Island Murder Victims"
22. "Inside the Long Island Serial Killer and Gilgo Beach"
23. "The Gilgo Beach Killer | Criminal Minds"
24. "In Long Island serial killer investigation, new phone technology may be key to break in case"

The Thawk E-mail Account was also used to search a number of podcasts and/or documentaries regarding this investigation, as well as repeatedly viewing hundreds of images depicting the murdered victims and members of their immediate families. Significantly, Rex Heuermann also searched for and viewed articles concerning the very Task Force that was investigating him.

Standing back from this apparently damning information, one could clearly say that Rex Heuermann surely *boxed* himself in (pun intended), referencing burner phone/cellphone coverage—assuming, of course, that the culprit is, indeed, the accused.

PHYSICAL EVIDENCE

December 11–13, 2010:

The remains of four young women were found along Ocean Parkway in a wooded area near Gilgo Beach. Male and female hairs were recovered. On December 11, 2010, Suffolk County police officer John Malia was conducting a training exercise with his canine partner, Blue, when the dog found a set of remains belonging to Melissa Barthelemy. On December 13, 2010, police found the remains of the three other women: Amber Lynn Costello, Maureen Brainard-Barnes, and Megan Waterman. Each of the four victims' bodies were examined by a forensic scientist at the Suffolk County Crime Laboratory. A female's hair, different from the victims, was found on three of the four bodies. The hairs were sent to an outside forensic laboratory. A male hair was also found on one of the victim's remains. The hair was unsuitable for DNA analysis at that time by the Suffolk County Crime Laboratory. Around this time, the police were searching for 24-year-old Shannan Gilbert, a sex worker from New Jersey, who vanished on May 1, 2010 after running from a client's house in Oak Beach. Her body was recovered 19 months later.

July 2020 (10 Years Later):

Mitochondrial DNA analysis, which was not as refined a decade earlier as it is today, was one of the major breakthroughs in helping to solve this crime. In brief, four female hairs were later tied to Heuermann's wife (Asa Ellerup), found on three of the Gilgo Four victims' bodies: two female hairs were recovered from Megan Waterman; one female hair was found on tape used to wrap burlap around Amber Lynn Costello that had been bound by three pieces of clear or white duct tape inside of burlap wrapping; one female hair was detected within a belt buckle found on Maureen Brainard-Barnes [one of three leather belts used to bind Barnes]. Although Rex Heuermann has not been charged with Barnes' murder, he is the prime suspect.

Additionally, a male hair was recovered from the bottom of the burlap used to wrap Megan Waterman.

July 31, 2020:

DNA profile generated from a male's hair found on one of the victim's remains was submitted for further forensics analysis. Forensic scientists generated a DNA profile from the hair recovered and determined that the hair belonged to a male in a mitochondrial haplogroup; that is, a population who share a similar mtDNA sequence. Because mitochondria are passed on only by women, no men (nor their ancestors) from whom one descends, they are encapsulated in the results.

Mitochondrial DNA is different from nuclear DNA. Nuclear DNA is inherited from both parents; mitochondrial DNA only from the mother. Therefore, all children from the same mother will share mitochondrial DNA (mtDNA).

According to the bail application presented to the court by the district attorney's office, prosecutors state that one hair was found on Maureen Brainard-Barnes, two were found on Megan Waterman, and another "piece of hair" was found on Amber Lynn Costello. But at the time the three women's remains were discovered in Long Island's

Gilgo Beach area in December 2010, the hairs "were not suitable for traditional nuclear DNA testing," said District Attorney Ray Tierney.

A mitochondrial DNA test can trace a person's maternal ancestry, but it needs a sample for comparison. "So, Suffolk County PD and the FBI surveilled Heuermann," Tierney said, "obtaining DNA samples from him and his wife off of objects they discarded.

"Now, we go back and we perform that analysis," Tierney continued. "Two out of the three hairs on Megan Waterman. One, that the mitochondrial DNA profile obtained from that hair matches the defendant. One other DNA profile on that hair matches his wife, such that over 99 percent of the rest of the population can be excluded," Tierney added. He also says the hair found on Amber Lynn Costello "matched the wife," as well.

On March 14, 2022, the Gilgo Beach Homicide Investigation Task Force had a *suspect*, Rex Heuermann, in their sights—and under constant surveillance as investigators built their case. On July 13, 2023, Heuermann was arrested and charged with three murders. In a matter of months, the task force team accomplished what the past administrations failed to resolve in thirteen years. And the investigation(s) continue.

Rex Andrew Heuermann was identified as a suspect after detectives linked him to the pickup truck that a witness reported seeing in 2010. Following the discovery of the Chevrolet Avalanche, which was registered to Heuermann, detectives began investigating cellphone records and other items. Heuermann made cellphone calls in the same location where burner phones were used. According to court records, Heuermann used his American Express Card in the same area where he used the burner phone to contact the victims. Heuermann also made calls from the same locations where he checked voicemails and called Melissa Barthelemy's family members.

Significantly, investigators could not find one instance when Heuermann was in a separate location from these other cellphones when such communication events occurred. Heuermann's Tinder account, linked to one of the burner phones that American Express records obtained via subpoena, revealed payments made by Heuermann to Tinder. According to records obtained from Tinder,

Heuermann, who went by the name Andy (using his middle name) in his Tinder profile, had links to a phone number which was connected to one of the burner phones. The burner phone was linked to an e-mail account. The account was created on January 15, 2011. A search warrant on the e-mail account revealed selfie photos taken by defendant Rex Heuermann. That burner e-mail account had many searches related to the Long Island serial killer. Another burner e-mail account was used to conduct thousands of searches related to sex workers, sadistic torture-related pornography, and child pornography. The e-mail account was also used to search active and known serial killers, the disappearance of Maureen Brainard-Barnes, Megan Waterman, Amber Lynn Costello, and a number of podcasts and documentaries about the investigation, including articles referencing the Task Force murder investigation.

July 2022:

In July of 2022, a DNA profile was generated referencing female hairs found on the remains of three bodies. Forensic scientists determined that each of the female hairs recovered from Maureen Brainard-Barnes, Megan Waterman, and Amber Lynn Costello belong to a female in the mitochondrial haplogroup A1C2. On July 21, 2022, an undercover detective recovered eleven bottles from a trash can in front of Heuermann's home. The Suffolk County Crime Laboratory took swabs of the bottles and sent them to a forensics laboratory for DNA profiling.

January 2023:

On January 26, 2023, authorities recover a pizza box, pizza crust, and a crumpled napkin thrown in a trash can outside Rex Heuermann's office building, allegedly belonging to Heuermann. The pizza box was sent to the Suffolk County Crime Laboratory for analysis.

February 24, 2023:

DNA profile on hairs match bottles linked to Heuermann's wife, Asa Ellerup.

March 23, 2023:

Suffolk County Crime Laboratory sent a swab from the pizza crust to another forensics laboratory. On April 28, 2023, a detective hand-delivered a portion of a male hair found on one of the victim's remains for forensics testing.

May 19, 2023:

Heuermann was captured on surveillance video purchasing minutes on one of the burner phones at a Midtown Manhattan store.

June 12, 2023:

A forensic laboratory determined the male hair found on one of the victims and the swab from the pizza crust had the same mitochondrial DNA profile. Rex Heuermann has been identified as the alleged killer.

July 13, 2023:

Heuermann was arrested in connection to three of the Gilgo Beach murders. His home and other locations were searched. Up until his arrest, Heuermann continued to use burner phones to contact sex workers. Since his arrest, Heuermann has been on suicide watch at the Riverhead Correctional Facility. As mentioned earlier, Heuermann was charged with three counts each of first-degree and second-degree murder.

August 4, 2023:

A 34-year-old Manhattan woman who worked as an escort at the time of her disappearance was identified as Karen Ann Vergata, brought up in Glenwood Landing, a hamlet on Long Island. Known as Fire Island Jane Doe #7, missing from February 14, 1996, when she last called her father from prison, was identified via genetic genealogy. The partial remains of two severed legs were first discovered on April 20, 1996 in a black plastic garbage bag floating in the water along Blue Point Beach, approximately one mile west of Fire Island's Davis Park. Fifteen years later in April of 2011, a second set of remains, inclusive of Vergata's skull, was found near Jones Beach along Ocean Parkway.

A retired homicide detective had contacted authorities and told them about the severed legs that had washed ashore in 1996. Vergata's remains had been safely stored away in a freezer at the medical examiner's office for more than fifteen years. In July of 2011, DNA testing revealed that the skull and legs belonged to the same person; however, it would be more than a decade before the victim could be positively identified. Eleven years later, in September of 2022, genetic genealogy was used to home in on the woman's identity.

August 16, 2023:

Heuermann had to submit to a buccal (cheek) swab test to bolster the prosecution's probable cause case against him. The test took place in the Riverhead Correctional Facility. The test would be used to compare a mitochondrial DNA profile developed from pizza crust and a used napkin allegedly discarded by Heuermann outside his Manhattan office. Results of the buccal swab came back as a match indicating that Rex had contact with victim Megan Waterman as well as the burlap used to restrain and transport her remains.

CHAPTER FOURTEEN

Let's take a close look at Rex Heuermann and his family. Heuermann started his architectural firm, RH Consultants & Associates, around the time he purchased the home he was raised in from his mother in 1994; that is, 29 years ago.

Rex was first married to the former Elizabeth R. Ryan in St, Peter's Church in New Brunswick, New Jersey, 1990. Elizabeth graduated from New York Institute of Technology, Westbury, Long Island, with a degree in architectural technology. She filed for divorce in 1995, which was finalized in 1996. The marriage deteriorated because of Rex Heuermann's infidelity, abuse, and obsession with online escorts. Note a familiar pattern?

Asa Ellerup (obviously keeping her maiden name), who is of Icelandic descent, was born in South Farmingdale, Long Island, New York in 1963. She, too, is 60 years old, married to Rex for 27 years. Her daughter Victoria Heuermann is 26; Victoria's stepbrother, Christopher Sheridan, is 33. Asa filed for divorce less than a week after her husband's arrest. Asa's attorney, Robert Macedonio, states that the decision to divorce her husband was mostly a precautionary measure to protect her from potential lawsuits stemming from families of the victims. Again, it is important to note that police say that Asa and her children were either out of town, state or country when the murders that Heuermann is charged with occurred. Police emphatically state that Asa Ellerup is in no way suspected of any wrongdoing. "They were completely blindsided by the event," states Police Commissioner Rodney Harrison.

Asa has been in phone contact with her husband, but the conversations have been kept very basic, both sides having been advised to limit their discussions as all phone calls are recorded.

Two storage units of Heuermann's were searched in Amityville, just 2.3 miles from his home. Ground-penetrating radar, a backhoe, and a dump truck were used in digging up the area and search the yard of the home. Three cadaver dogs were also brought in. It was a major excavation. At the end of the search, all that a closed-mouthed investigative team would reveal was the search proved "fruitful."

The fact that authorities found some 279 guns in a vault in Rex Heuermann's home does not scream out serial killer. Donna and I have been to a couple's home where the man, a serious gun collector, has several hundred weapons. However, several hairs found on the bodies of three of the four victims connecting Rex Heuermann to those crimes speak volumes. In a way, it's a bit ironic that the transference of his wife's own hair in three instances already helped seal her husband's fate. Keep in mind, too, that one of the male hairs found on Megan Waterman is a match to Rex Heuermann. Technological advancements in mitochondrial DNA analysis are only warming up, helping to solve a good many cold-case murders. Setting that fact aside for the moment, I cannot emphasize enough the sheer fact that authorities under the James Burke / Thomas Spota / Christopher McPartland regime [christened "The Administration" as they quietly referred to themselves], could have had Rex Heuermann in their sights as early as September of 2010. Thirteen years ago.

In the winter of 2010, Dave Schaller, Amber Lynn Costello's pimp, clearly brought evidence of this fact before the police on *more* than one occasion. That witness had not only given detectives a description of the vehicle the man was driving that evening, he gave them a very accurate description of the stranger's (Heuermann) distinguishing features: "Ogre-like looking, 6 foot 4 inches tall, weighing approximately 240 pounds." What was only brought to the attention of the public most recently was that Schaller had reportedly told detectives that he even exchanged blows with the perspective client after coming home and pretending to be furious at finding Costello locked in the bathroom. "When the police told me she was dead, he [the client] was the first person who jumped into my head. I've been picturing his face for 13 years," Costello's pimp told the *Associated Press*.

I only first read about that part of the story detailing the fight between the two men published in the AP on July 23, 2023. The piece was headlined **Dave Schaller came face to face with alleged Gilgo Beach serial killer Rex Heuermann; 12 years later, his tip helped crack the case.** The fact that Dave Schaller had initially given a full description of both the vehicle and the man to the police shortly after Amber Lynn Costello's disappearance shows that the eyewitnesses' statement fell on deaf ears.

Addressing the matter following Rex Heuermann's arrest, Dave Schaller voiced his anger and frustration, explaining one of his last meetings with homicide detectives approximately two years after Costello went missing. "I gave them the exact description of the truck and the dude. I mean, come on; why didn't they use that?" Schaller had identified the first-generation Chevrolet Avalanche vehicle model from a line-up of photographs.

Suffolk County Legislator Rob Trotta, who had worked as a Suffolk County detective until 2013, said "This was crucial information, and I don't know why they didn't share it."

Also reported from the *Associated Press* article: "Two high-ranking officials who worked closely on the case and attended briefings between 2011 and 2013 said they never heard anything about a witness statement describing the subject and his vehicle."

Amazing! Amazing until you stop and realize that you had a past administration hellbent on turning a blind eye for reasons cited throughout these pages; that is, an administration comprised of Thomas Spota, James Burke, Christopher McPartland, and several others serving on the outer fringes of the inner circle.

Of interesting note is that serial killers generally start murdering in their early 20s and 30s. Rex Heuermann would have been in his mid-forties when the Gilgo Four were murdered. It's highly unlikely that Heuermann started killing at that stage of his life, which is to say that he may likely have killed several to many times before. Food for thought.

Standing back from the whole business, it remains unarguable that the Rodney Harrison, Ray Terney, Gilgo Beach Homicide Investigation

Task Force team accomplished in a matter of a year and a half what the prior administration failed to do in thirteen years. That is, affect the arrest of The Long Island Serial Killer (or at least one of them). The prior administration knowingly thwarted the investigation from the onset for reasons clearly set forth in this accounting. Christopher McPartland was the administration's architect of fabrication, putting the required spin on any number of particularly serious predicaments in which the trio found themselves. The corruption did not initiate in 2011, but rather starting in 1979 when a young Jimmy Burke first testified as the star witness for then prosecutor Thomas Spota in the Johnny Pius trial, addressed at the beginning of this profile.

No sooner than we find ourselves in the middle of sorting through this messy business, the disgraced police chief Jimmy Burke pops back into the picture, arrested once again.

On Tuesday morning of August 22, 2023 at 10:00 a.m., Jimmy Burke finds himself in handcuffs during an undercover sting operation at the Suffolk County Vietnam Veterans Memorial Park in Farmingville. The Suffolk County Park Rangers' Targeted Response Unit took Jimmy into custody for "soliciting for sexual engagement" explained Police Commissioner Rodney Harrison. Burke "attempted to use his former law enforcement status—and an appeal for sympathy due to the substance of the allegations—to avoid being arrested," officials stated. Burke said, "Do you know who I am?" The ranger who made the arrest did not at first know who Burke was until he identified himself. "He was expressing to us how this would be a public humiliation for him and such," said Sergeant Brian Quattrini, another park ranger.

Burke had a small amount of marijuana along with a muscle relaxant on his person but was not charged with a drug count. He was taken to the Sixth Precinct in Selden for processing, charged with offering a sex act, indecent exposure, public lewdness, and fifth degree criminal solicitation, then released with a desk appearance ticket and was due in court on September 11. 2023.

The *Daily Mail* (a British newspaper and news website published in London) gave a more detailed accounting regarding Jimmy Burke's words and actions with an undercover male park ranger that morning. The paper stated, "The former top cop is accused of pulling down his pants and displaying his genitals, as well as manipulating them in a sexual manner. He then reportedly told the undercover ranger, 'I like sucking dick.'"

In *Newsday*'s piece headlined **Former Suffolk Chief of Police James Burke charged with sexual solicitation**, the article pauses for a single isolated sentence to state that "Burke remains a notorious figure on Long Island." That pronouncement is an understatement.

Interestingly, a week after Burke's arrest for soliciting sex from a male park ranger as part of a sting operation at Suffolk County Vietnam Veterans Memorial Park in Farmingville, two of the four original charges were suddenly dropped. Burke was ultimately charged with 'public lewdness' and 'indecent exposure.' "This decision was made by the county after discussions with Suffolk police detectives," said Suffolk County spokeswoman Marykate Guilfoyle. A more thorough explanation is that the top two charges of 'offering a sex act' and 'criminal solicitation' were dropped because Burke did not offer money, and there was no discussion of monies being exchanged. The two charges must go hand in hand.

As an aside, this accounting is somewhat reminiscent of Long Island's Joey Buttafuoco character, who lands in trouble with the law, does jail time, moves to California, solicits an undercover female cop, winding up in Double Trouble. Incidentally, that was the name of Joey's boat. Joey Buttafuoco was and is a sex addict. Jimmy Burke was and is a sex addict on multiple fronts. The only difference is that Joey is just plain trouble whereas Jimmy is plainly dangerous.

Another curious observation was that the Buttafuoco home was just 3 miles away from the Heuermann home, when in May of 1992, 17-year-old Amy Fisher, Joey's lover, shot Joey's wife, Mary Jo Buttafuoco, on the porch of their Massapequa home. Not to mention that Heuermann's home is less than 9 miles from 1993 convicted serial killer Joel Rifkin's East Meadow residence. Backing up in time to the Amityville Horror murders of December 1975, Ronald Joseph DeFeo Jr. of 112 Ocean Avenue, systematically shot and killed six family members: father, mother, two brothers, and two sisters. The distance between the Amityville home and Heuermann's home in Massapequa

Park is less that 3 miles. Some folks jokingly say that the bizarre coincidences are connected to the water. ☺ Others who say there are no coincidences claim it's the Kool Aid. ☺ I feel that a bit of levity is in order after a grueling yet successful 18-month ordeal in identifying and building a case against Rex Heuermann on behalf of the investigative task force. Yes? And there is so much more to come.

A reminder: Following the incident where former Chief of Police Jimmy Burke severely beat prisoner Christopher Loeb at the Fourth Precinct in Smithtown, Detective Lieutenant James Hickey was the government's star witness in the case against Spota and McPartland for covering up the assault. After receiving a federal subpoena to testify in the Loeb case, Burke met Hickey alone in a restaurant parking lot. "I was very concerned he wanted to kill me if I testified," Hickey said of Burke.

There is still a good deal of speculation that Jimmy Burke may in some way be involved with the serial killings. But as Heuermann is now charged with first- and second-degree murder in three of the Gilgo Beach victims, as well as their prime suspect in a fourth, perhaps that speculation has somewhat shifted. However, you'll recall that people who knew James Burke well were asked if the police chief could be a possible serial killer, a former police officer and a once good friend of Burke's succinctly stated, "He has that vibe." Also, former Suffolk County District Attorney Tim Sini at the time stated that "James Burke is proffered a suspect" in the LISK investigation.

Following Jimmy Burke's rearrest on August 22, 2023 for soliciting sex from a male park ranger as part of a sting operation, Attorney John Ray is calling for an investigation of Burke into the murder of a still unidentified Asian male known as John Doe #8, found along Ocean Parkway in April of 2011. He suffered massive trauma to the skull, which was possibly the result of gunshot wounds; the only body of the ten that was discovered with conceivable bullet devastation.

Calling for an investigation of Burke in this matter is not unreasonable when considering what we have learned and are learning about this disgraced cop as we pursue a deviant path that has often been brushed aside.

We learn that Burke ran a prostitution ring with Lowrita Rickenbacker and later Heather Malone. We learn that the ring was comprised of both female and male prostitutes. We learn of his own leanings in procuring prostitutes and consuming drugs at cocaine-fueled sex parties in the area where the Gilgo Beach bodies were found. Even while serving time in federal prison for assaulting Christopher Loeb, Burke is found with oxycodone in his foot locker. We later learn that Burke is a cross-dresser. We learn that he is bisexual. We learn that Thomas Spota, Jimmy Burke, and Christopher McPartland referred to themselves as the "The Administration" and considered themselves untouchable. We learn that the trio used the power of their positions to threaten their perceived enemies with radical demotions and career-ending false criminal charges. We learn that Spota went to great lengths to protect a very troubled Jimmy Burke. We're reminded that a disgraced Jimmy Burke nevertheless receives an annual pension of $145,485.

Backing up for a moment, on August 11, 2023, John Ray was very vocal in calling out Asa Ellerup as having everyone conned, initially receiving food stamps when her husband makes very good money and owns property in several states. As of this writing, she has collected $55K through a GoFundMe page. Ray goes on to state that her husband is in the downstairs basement with sex workers, having spent a fortune for their services.

John Ray points to DNA evidence found at the crime scene, stating that two out of the three hairs recovered from the wrappings of the victims' bodies belong to Asa Ellerup. "That alone puts her in the circle of suspicion," said Ray. "I do not say that she was seen killing anybody. I say that she was present in the home and knew very well that this man [her husband] had a long series for years of prostitutes coming to his home and paying them while she was there upstairs and present when some of this is happening," Ray said during a Saturday appearance on *News Nation Prime*.

"Asa Ellerup should be considered a suspect and not just a bystander or someone who's been victimized by her husband," Ray said in an interview with the *New York Daily News*.

"She is complicit in her husband's solicitation and use of sex workers in his home over the course of years," John Ray stated during an appearance on *News Nation*'s Chris CUOMO show.

Since Rex Heuermann's arrest, Asa made no indication of sympathy for the victims' families.

John Ray claims he has a very credible witness attesting to the fact that Asa was well-aware that her husband was frequently bringing sex workers home over the course of years and that Asa was herself actively involved at times. "I tested the witness using the usual tests for truth, and she tested out fine."

When challenged by a *News Nation* interviewer that Asa Ellerup has been cleared by the police of any wrongdoing, citing that Asa was out of town during the murders, Ray responded with, "Those out-of-town visits could be fungible. She really needs to be a suspect because we don't know how long the victims were kept, or how long he had them before they were buried. We don't know any of these things."

If what John Ray is saying is true, or more accurately if his witness is telling the truth, it puts Asa Ellerup's alibi in a new light. The fact that she was out of town, state, or country at the times her husband allegedly committed the murders is moot, as investigators themselves, in essence, provided her with that alibi. The transference of the evidentiary hairs recovered from the victims' bodies seems more plausible when considering this new information. Of course, skepticism abounds since Ray is playing this close to the vest at this point.

"John Ray is trying to keep himself relevant in this case," insists Robert Macedonio, attorney for Asa Ellerup. "This mystery witness does not exist. I can assure you Ellerup was not involved in this, knew nothing about it."

Vess Mitev, the attorney for Ellerup's two adult children said that Ray's accusations are "a disservice" to the victims in this case.

In terms of monetary wealth, it is reported that Rex Heuermann helped oversee projects costing over 68 million dollars in the decades leading up to his arrest, according to the New York City Department of

Buildings filings. He was an expert expeditor, navigating clients through the arcane business of city building codes rather than architectural design. His fees would be in the range of 10% to 15%. That would conservatively put net profits somewhere in the area of $6,800,000. His monthly office rent is estimated at four figures plus utilities, subtracted from what he pays in employee salaries. Couple an arbitrary figure to untold property assets and a gun collection valued at some $300.000, and you'll realize the man is not a pauper. It is said that Heuermann spent a small fortune on escort services. Still, it appears that he had quite a bit of discretionary income. It may be of interest to note that his office is staffed with young, petite, attractive women. A rather subjective observation, but worth mention.

Referencing the GoFundMe page set up by Melissa Moore, the daughter of the "Happy Face Killer," serial killer Keith Hunter Jesperson, convicted in 1995 of raping and murdering eight women, Melissa's heart is in the right place. She wants to help Asa Ellerup and her children rebuild their home and repair the damage caused by the investigators during the twelve-day search conducted of the Heuermann home.

Asa Ellerup and her children returned home to litter boxes from three cats strewn about, pictures thrown all over the place, a couch completely shredded, other couches and mattresses removed from the home, no bed to sleep in, dresser drawers emptied, a vinyl bathtub cut open, floors ripped up, piles of debris everywhere, barely any place to walk.

On September 3, 2023, John Ray told the *Daily Mail* that several sources have contacted him over the past month saying they had previously encountered Rex Heuermann roaming the area [colloquially known as 'pickle park'] looking for casual sex." The park area of mention is where Jimmy Burke was busted the prior month on August 22, 2023 for offering oral sex to a male park ranger as part of a sting operation. Vietnam Veteran's Memorial Park in Farmingville is but one of many cruising grounds known for 'gay cruising.' Gay cruising is defined as walking or driving around the area looking for casual sex from an anonymous male partner.

John Ray is urging the Suffolk County police to investigate any possible social connection between Jimmy Burke and Rex Heuermann, emphasizing the high probability that their overall sexual predilections could have brought them into contact with one another. Both men led an extensive double life, covering a gamut of sexual activity.

Those who shared certain information with John Ray referencing Rex Heuermann and not the police did so because they have real concerns, especially in having their families finding out about their own sexual preferences, the attorney explained.

Rex Heuermann's brother, Craig Heuermann, presently lives in Chester, South Carolina. In 1988, Craig was living in Massapequa Park when he was involved in a vehicular accident that claimed the life of City Housing Police Captain Winnion Buskey. Craig was drunk and "coked up" when he crashed into a vehicle on the Southern State Parkway. He had a blood alcohol level of .20, twice the legal limit. Too, Craig had a blood cocaine level of .05. He pleaded guilty to criminally negligent homicide and was sentenced to three years; it is reported that he received five years probation. In another reported incident, after moving to Chester, Craig attacked a neighbor with a pipe or pole because the man was cutting his grass on a Sunday.

Police in Rock Hill, South Carolina are looking to connect Rex Heuermann to the disappearance of an 18-year-old local woman who went missing from her home two days before Thanksgiving in 2014. "Aaliyah Bell disappeared just 20 miles away from a property Rex Heuermann owns in Chester," said Rock Hill Police Lieutenant Michael Chavis. "So far there is no indication that leads us to identify Rex Heuermann as a suspect in this case," Chavis added. "We will continue to investigate Bell's disappearance and follow up on all tips and leads."

Aaliyah Bell

Another South Carolina woman, 37-year-old Julia Ann Bean, suddenly vanished on May 31, 2017, the day before her daughter Cameron's high school graduation.

"I gave her three tickets [to my graduation]" Cameron related in a text to the *Sun*, "just in case she lost one, and I gave him [allegedly Rex Heuermann] two so he could bring her. He told me he has lake houses and big boats if I ever wanted to have a boat party. He offered to take me to a concert and told me he wanted to marry my mom. I never saw her again after that night."

When Cameron saw Rex Heuermann on the news following his arrest, she said she "had chills," saying she recognized him right away. "That was the last man I saw her with personally," Cameron said. Heuermann had arrived earlier in a dark truck with her mom and introduced himself by a different name.

A friend of the victim, Heidi Kovas, says she has been talking about Julia since the day she disappeared six years ago. When she saw the Gilgo Beach victims on the news she said her "jaw dropped." Kovas said, "All of them matched Julia. Everything. The blonde hair, the green eyes, the fact Julia was so petite." She said that Cameron also knew right away.

Julia Ann Bean had left all her personal items at home the day she disappeared: wallet, keys, cellphone, money in her purse, drugs left on the table. Cameron recalls that the man was driving a truck.

Scott Bonner, an investigator with the Sumter County Sherrif's office said they're investigating the potential connection to Rex Heuermann.

Julia Ann Bean

Additionally, Las Vegas, Nevada police, where Rex Heuermann has a time-share, have been scouring their missing person records for ties to Rex Heuermann. Heuermann had planned to retire to his secluded undeveloped 18-acre plot of land in Chester, South Carolina (which he purchased in 2021), and live near his brother Craig's property, which is situated just across the road. Neighbors say the brothers planned to buy up much of the property in the area and build a "compound." Chester is a small rural city approximately 50 miles southwest of Charlotte, North Carolina.

Rex Heuermann has a valued $800,000 property portfolio listed among his Las Vegas, Nevada time-share ~ Club de Soleil ($16,995); 4 vacant lots in Chester, South Carolina ($154,000); and a home in Massapequa Park, Long Island, New York ($650,000). Chester, South Carolina is 80 miles northwest of Sumter County, where Julia Bean lived when she was last seen.

Investigators are searching for clues that may possibly link Rex Heuermann to four victims found in the Mojave Desert. When you are looking at the Mojave Desert as a whole, you are dealing with 25,000 square miles. It can be daunting because you have four states that border this vast tract of land: southeast California, Nevada, Arizona, Utah.

In 2004, Rex Heuermann bought a time-share at Club Wyndham Grand Desert, 265 East Harmon Avenue, Las Vegas, Nevada. He sold this property in 2013. The time-share is just east of the Las Vegas Strip (Las Vegas Boulevard). In 2005, Heuermann bought a two-bedroom time-share at Club de Soleil, 5499 West Tropicana Avenue, just three miles west of the Las Vegas Strip. Being that Victoria Camara's body was found 26 miles southeast of Las Vegas puts Heuermann's residences in the vicinity.

Five victims in question were discovered between 2003 and 2006.

Misty Marie Saens: On March 12, 2003, 25-year-old Misty Marie Saens disappeared from Las Vegas. Her torso was found wrapped in black plastic bags and bed sheets. Misty's partial remains were found in the desert on a road leading to Red Rock Canyon National Conservation Area, just east of the Las Vegas Strip.

Misty Marie Saens

Victoria Camera: On August 11, 2003, 17-year-old Victoria Camera's body was found near a desert haul road in Boulder City, Nevada, dumped like trash 26 miles southeast of Las Vegas.

Victoria Camera

Jodi Marie Brewer: On August 29, 2003, Las Vegas resident Jodi Marie Brewer's torso was found wrapped in cloth and plastic, discovered across the state line in San Bernadino County, California. Her torso had been cut with precision using a surgical saw.

Jodi Marie Brewer

Lindsay Marie Harris: On May 4, 2005, Lindsay Marie Harris, 21 years old, disappeared from her home in Henderson, Nevada. She was last seen at a nearby bank making a deposit. Her rental car was found abandoned in the desert at the southern end of the Valley. Nineteen days later, on May 23, 2005, human legs were discovered in a grassy field off Interstate 55 in Divernon, Illinois. After conducting DNA testing, it was learned that both legs belonged to the same person. Three years later, in May 2008, the FBI matched DNA samples of the unknown Illinois victim to Lindsay Harris. Rex Heuermann is under investigation in Harris' murder. Heuermann and his wife had purchased the Club de Soleil time-share on April 23, 2005; 11 days before Lindsay disappeared.

Lindsay Marie Harris

Jessica Edith Louise Foster: On March 28, 2006, 21-year-old Jessica Edith Louise Foster was last seen in Las Vegas, Nevada. She is still missing as of this writing, October 2023. Jessica last had phone contact with her family while she was at her home in the 1000 block of Cornerstone Place in North Las Vegas.

Jessica Edith Louise Foster

In late September 2023, at a hearing outside the courtroom, Rex Heuermann's defense attorney, Michael Brown, downplayed a piece of highly incriminating evidence against his client referencing a near perfect DNA match of a hair sample recovered from a victim and one analyzed and compared with a buccal swab from Heuermann's cheek, proving that it was Heuermann's DNA.

Yet, Brown sallied with, "There is nobody on the face of the earth that is credible who is going to say that hair is my client's hair. It's impossible under science standards. What they can do is say he could potentially be a donor for that hair, but so could thousands and thousands of other people in our area, so take that for what it's worth."

Really? Does Michael Brown not realize that DNA testing is 99-plus-proof positive?

Bail Application from District Attorney Ray Tierney's Office:

"Forensic Laboratory #2. On or about March 23, 2023, the Suffolk County Crime Laboratory requested Forensic Laboratory #2, a lab specializing in forensic mitochondrial analysis, to conduct additional, independent analyses. On or about June 12, 2023, Forensic Laboratory #2 issued a report concluding that the DNA sample from the female recovered from the bottles outside the residence of Defendant Heuermann (i.e., Heuermann's wife) and the Female Hair on Costello indicated that the mitochondrial DNA profile(s) are the same at all compared positions common to and between samples, specifically at a rate that would exclude 99.98% of the North American population from the Female Hair on Costello.

"Forensic Laboratory #2 then compared the profile associated with the DNA sample from Heuermann's wife to one of the two aforementioned female hairs recovered on the remains of Ms. Waterman, which also resulted in the conclusion that the "mitochondrial DNA profile(s) are the same at all compared positions common to and between samples," specifically at a rate that would exclude 99.69% of the North American population from the hair recovered on Ms. Waterman. Based on the foregoing, while 99.98% of the North American population can be excluded from the FEMALE HAIR ON COSTELLO and 99.69% of the North American population are excluded from the FEMALE HAIR ON WATERMAN, it is significant that Rex Heuermann's wife cannot be excluded from either the female hairs recovered on the remains of Megan Waterman and Amber Lynn Costello."

To say that authorities are leaving no stone unturned is *pretty much* an understatement. I say "pretty much" because the police, even with the creation of the newly formed Gilgo Beach Homicide Investigation Task Force holding to the story that Shannon Gilbert's death was the result of a "misadventure" in lieu of a murder, that she likely drowned in Oak Beach after calling 911 for help, stating, "They're trying to kill me," I firmly believe she was murdered.

Let's hear what Attorney John Ray for the Shannan Gilbert family had to say on that matter when interviewed by Julie Grant of Court TV on October 4, 2023, titled **New Evidence in Rex Heuermann Case Could Lead to Serial Killings.**

Julie Grant: I'd like to begin by asking you, John, as you have been running your own parallel investigation so to speak, using private investigators to ascertain any available information about Shannan's disappearance, has there been anything new learned since we last checked in with you?

John Ray: There's an enormous amount of new information and evidence that we've learned. All of the evidence and the new evidence that we have points to the same thing inexorably. That is, that Shannan was murdered. It reaches the point where the police's facile story is not just a fable but an absurd fable when you consider all of the evidence, and I can't believe they're adhering to that story up until now. Perhaps that's changing, but there's no evidence of it.

Julie Grant: What is the police's story of the circumstances of Shannan's death?

John Ray: I don't believe that they believe their own story, but their story is that Shannan became crazed by some unknown cause, ran into an almost impenetrable marsh as daylight was about to come up, and found her way into the marsh, a relatively narrow marsh, and just managed to drop dead. And the other theory they espouse equally is that she died from drowning, where she's found face up by the bush, and there's no water even close by. She would have to drink the water in order to drown. And yet they adhere to this absurdity. Why? I have a problem with that.

Julie Grant: In these investigations that you've been involved with privately, has there been any indications of any involvement with Rex Heuermann?

John Ray: Yes, there have been. The details of that I'm not ready to disclose. I've attempted to work with and have had some cooperation with the police department on this new evidence that's developed. But now, for the first time, there's a real strong possibility that Heuermann was connected with the group of people who are responsible for the death of Shannan Gilbert. We've always maintained that when you hear that tape, you'll see that I'm right, that there's a group of people involved. Not just one. And that's why Shannan says, "*<u>They're</u>* trying to kill me." The people who contact me are able to make a synapse between Heuermann's life and the lives of those at Oak Beach. So, we'll see. That's unfolding. It's going to take an enormous amount of intense investigation to put those synapses together and make them tight; but they do exist. Part of the reason that this kind of information has come to us is that people/witnesses from all different places in the country have been calling me who are afraid to speak to the police or have reasons not to want to speak to the police. They call and speak to me, and I give them time. I put in the effort and meet them. It helps advance this whole thing.

Keep in mind that the police to this very day maintain Shannan Gilbert *may have been* in a drug-induced and/or alcoholic state of mind, exacerbated by a bipolar condition as she fled from client Joseph Brewer's home in Oak Beach. Also, one could come away with the conclusion that Shannan was sober and as sane as a judge, compounded solely by a combination of confusion melded with sheer fear as she ran screaming for her life! Take your pick—or listen carefully between the lines. Listening to those 911 tapes, one could easily come away with either conclusion or an amalgamation of both interpretations.

We'll have to wait until Rex Heuermann's trial to learn the full details of these investigations, which will likely take years. Keep in mind one important fact: According to FBI profiling, serial killers begin their murderous acts in their early to mid-twenties. Rex Heuermann would have been in his mid-forties when the Gilgo Four were murdered. Therefore, it is highly probable that Heuermann had murdered others decades earlier in time. Hence, authorities have expanded their search for clues prior to 2007—including several states throughout the country.

Standing back from it all, it is perhaps ironic to note that Thomas Spota and Jimmy Burke (later Christopher McPartland), who for decades destroyed the lives of so many along the way, in the end, dismantled their own lives as well.

No sooner than I put this book to bed on October 18, 2023, Attorney John Ray held a press conference with Police Commissioner Rodney

Harrison. Immediately, that should tell you that the Gilgo Beach Homicide Investigation Task Force team is taking John Ray seriously referencing the allegations he made earlier concerning witnesses that he held in abeyance who could shed new light on the police investigations. And what a light Ray cast. In a word, extraordinary!

Commissioner Harrison confirmed that they are, indeed, interviewing four new witnesses who could connect more cases to suspect Rex Heuermann. "When it comes to Miss Karen Vergata, and when it comes to Miss Shannan Gilbert, they're the ones that we are going to take a closer look at and see if they are connected to our defendant," Harrison said.

Standing next to Ray, Harrison said that his office is interviewing four new potential witnesses who first came forward to John Ray, attorney for the Gilbert family.

One of the witnesses, a female banker by day, and a taxi cab driver by night, signed an affidavit stating that she picked up Shannan Gilbert in the fall of 2009, who had been hiding in the Sayville Lodge motel bathroom as the man she recognized as Rex Heuermann fled the scene.

John Ray relates part of that story: "Suddenly, a giant man who fits the description of Rex Heuermann comes out of the motel, covering his face with his arms so he can't be identified. He runs to a van or an SUV that's parked nearby. The taxi driver continues to flash her lights and beep her horn as part of a prearranged signal with the dispatcher until Shannan runs out, crying, shaking, very upset, and gets in the taxi," Ray explains.

Another witness in sworn testimony said that she and her boyfriend were swingers, belonging to La Trapeze, a club based in Midtown Manhattan, close to where Heuermann worked as an architect. She said that Heuermann in 1996 had posted on the wall of La Trapeze a notice asking for a sexual encounter at his Massapequa Park home. The witness' swinger boyfriend was a NYPD narcotics detective, referred to in the affidavit as R.W. In February of 1996, R.W. and she picked up Karen Vergata in New York City, on their way to the Heuermann home. "Karen had just gotten out of jail; she was disheveled, hungry, and homeless," said the witness.

R.W., Karen, and she entered the Heuermann home and met Heuermann's wife, who was not only privy to the situation but was to be a participant, until seeing that the female witness is African American, to which Asa Ellerup declines.

"Karen went downstairs," the female witness wrote. "I stayed upstairs. My partner, who is bisexual, kept disappearing. I believe he was elsewhere in the house, having sex with Rex. I had sex with Rex as well. I never went downstairs."

The witness said that she had serviced Rex Heuermann many times in the past and that he was a serial user of sex workers. He would sometimes have them come to his house two at a time while his wife was home upstairs, Ray related. The witness said they left Karen Vergata playing "swinger games" with Rex Heuermann.

Once outside, the witness questioned her detective boyfriend as to why they were leaving Karen behind, who then suddenly ran naked and crying from the home. "He told me not to worry about her, that she was okay, that they were only playing a game. We left without her. I felt uneasy that we left without Karen." That was the last time the witness ever saw the woman.

Ray stated that the four witnesses who have come forward in the serial killer case have no agenda.

Harrison added, "We have a job here as law enforcement, as the Suffolk County Police Department, to make sure we investigate every single complaint or interest in this case, make sure we look under every single stone to see if there is any connection to Rex Heuermann, or if there is a connection to somebody else that may be involved with the bodies that were discovered on Ocean Parkway."

I, as the author, am confident that we are going to see a good many more dots connected in this serial killer case as time passes.

SOURCES

Adler, Dan, "We're Only Just Starting to Unpack Rex Heuermann's New York," *Vanity Fair*, August 7, 2023.

Alexander, Harriet and Connor Boyd Health, "Exclusive: Experts split as bone-like fragments are dug up from Gilgo Beach serial killer suspect Rex Heuermann's backyard – as they claim human remains can't be ruled out," *DailyMail.com*, July 25, 2023.

Asbury, John; Nicole Fuller, Grant Parpan, "Gilgo Beach Killings: Search of suspect Rex Heuermann's house is over, DA Ray Tierney says," *Newsday*, July 25, 2023.

Asbury, John; Robert Brodsky, Michael O'Keeffe, Grant Parpan and Ted Phillips, "Gilgo Beach Killings: Wife of accused serial killer Rex Heuermann pleads for privacy to 'regain normalcy' in neighborhood," *Newsday*, July 29, 2023.

Bashinsky and Alice Wright, "Gilgo Beach Serial Killer Suspect's Next-Door Neighbor of 15 Years Claims He Heard Rex Heiermann Digging in the Backyard in the Early Hours of the Morning and Smelled him Burning Trash 'every two weeks' – as Forensics are Seen Trawling Through Garden," *DailyMail.com*, July 21, 2023.

Beyrer, Kevin Lieutenant, Suffolk County 911 calls made by Shannan Gilbert. Video

Blass, Greg, "Was L.I. serial killer investigation stymied in cover-up by corrupt Suffolk cop and DA? We need a special prosecutor to probe investigation," *RiverheadLOCAL.com*, October 17, 2021.

Brodsky, Robert, "Arrest in Gilgo case 'a shocker,'" *Newsday*, July 15, 2023.

Brown, Lee, "Rex Heuermann Probes Now Span Several States, Las Vegas Cops Latest to Review Cold Case," *New York Post*, July 19, 2023.

Celona, Jerry and Jorge Fitz-Gibbon, "Long Island Cops Ignored Vital Lead that Could Have Led to Rex Heuermann 13 Years Ago," *New York Post,* July 18, 2023.

Chayes, Matthew, "Gilgo Beach Killings: What to Know About Rex Heuermann's Business Records," *Newsday*, July 31, 2023.

Chayes, Matthew, Nicole Fuller, Michael O'Keeffe and Grant Parpan, "Gilgo Beach killings: Investigators have identified 'Fire Island Jane Doe' as Karen Vergata," *Newsday*, August 4, 2023.

Cramer, Maria; William K. Rashbaum, Joseph Goldstein and Corey Kilgannon, "Officials Details Investigation into Gilgo Killings," *New York Times*, July 14, 2023.

Crane, Emily, "Former escort claims disgraced ex- Long Island police chief James Burke forced her into oral sex," *New York Post*, September 10, 2023.

DeStephano, Anthony, "Gilgo Beach Murder Case: Evolving DNA technology provides break," *Newsday*, July 19, 2023.

DeStefano, Anthony M., Nicole Fuller, Michael O'Keeffe, Grant Parpan and Sandra Peddie, " Gilgo Beach Killings: Exclusive interview with Suffolk County District Attorney Ray Tierney, *Newsday*, August 3, 2023.

DeStefano, Anthony M., Nicole Fuller, Michael O'Keeffe, Grant Parpan, Sandra Peddie and Craig Schneider, "Suspected Gilgo Beach killer Rex Heuermann engaged in 'disturbing' activity in months before his arrest, Suffolk Police Commissioner Rodney Harrison said," *Newsday*, August 9, 2023.

DeStefano, Anthony M., "Gilgo Beach killings: City ME used 9/11 techniques to help with Gilgo Beach cases, officials say," *Newsday,* August 26, 2023.

DeStefano, Anthony M., "Gilgo Beach Killings: Investigators zeroing in on Valerie Mack, Karen Vergata, and other victims in Rex Heuermann case," *Newsday*, October 16, 2023.

Eberhart, Chris, "Missing South Carolina woman last seen with Gilgo Beach murder suspect Rex Heuermann," *Fox News*, August 25, 2023.

Elassar, Alaa, "What Causes Someone to Become a Serial Killer? It's a Malignant Combination of Factors, experts say," *CNN*, July 24, 2023.

Faberov, Snejana, "Ex- escort Recounts Chilling Date with Accused Gilgo Beach Serial Killer Rex Heuermann," *New York Post*, July 19, 2023.

Firstman, Richard, and Jay Salpeter, *A Criminal Injustice*, Ballantine Books, 2008.

Fitz-Gibbon, Jorge "Cops Probe Rex Heiermann Link to South Carolina Missing Woman Case," *New York Post*, July 20, 2023.

Fuller, Nicole, Gus Garcia-Roberts, "Commish: 'A Demon That Walks Among Us,'" *Newsday*, July 15, 2023.

Fuller, Nicole, Michael O'Keeffe and Grant Parpan, "Prosecutors turn over thousands of pages of documents, evidence at accused Gilgo Beach serial killer Rex Heuermann's court appearance," *Newsday*, August 2, 2023.

Fuller, Nicole, Michael O'Keeffe and Grant Parpan, "Gilgo Beach killings: Investigators have identified 'Jane Dow No. 7,' source says," *Newsday*, August 4, 2023.

Fuller, Nicole and Grant Parpan, "Gilgo Beach killings: Prosecutors seek cheek swab from suspect Rex A. Heuermann for more DNA testing, court papers show," *Newsday*, August 2, 2023.

Fuller, Nicole, Michael O'Keeffe and Grant Parpan, "Prosecutors to rely on DNA, cellphone records and other evidence to make their case against serial killer Rex Heuermann, experts say," *Newsday*, August 12, 2023.

Garcia-Roberts, *Jimmy the King*, Public Affairs, 2022.

Halff, Noa, "Daughter of Julia Ann Bean says she last say her mom with Gilgo Beach serial killer suspect Rex Heuermann the day before she went missing in South Carolina and begs the cops to investigate," *DailyMail.com*, August 22, 2023.

Harrington, Mark and Sandra Peddie, "Gilgo Beach killings: Defense lawyers offer ways to challenge evidence in case against Rex Heuermann," *Newsday*, August 12, 2023.

Heal, Alexandra, "Gilgo Beach killer hunt showed infighting between prosecutors, police," *The Washington Post*, August 1, 2023.

James, Emma and Ruth Bashinsky "Disgraced Long Island police chief James Burke who botched serial killer Rex Heuermann probe is seen leaving jail after busted for 'offering male undercover cop oral sex' at 10 a,m, in prostitution sting," *DailyMail.com*, August 23, 3023.

Jensen, Bill and Alexis Linkletter, "Long Island Serial Killer," Podcast:
https://www.investigationdiscovery.com/crimefeed/podcasts/unraveled--long-island-serial-killer (ongoing).

Kenton, Luke, "Gilgo Beach suspect Rex Heuermann's children break silence on if they'll contact father after 'horrific' details emerge," *The U.S. Sun*, August 9, 2023.

Kenton, Luke, " Gilgo suspect Rex Heuermann's full body count may never be known & his Google searches point to two killers, expert says," *The U.S. Sun*, August 12, 2023.

________, Gilgo Beach victim's lawyer wants disgraced op James Burke investigated for Asian male's 'LISK murder' after his arrest," *The U.S. Sun*, August 25, 2023.

Land, Olivia, "Billy Baldwin in Slayers Class" *New York Post*, July 15, 2023.

Land, Olivis, "'Average Joe' suspect: 'Sometimes I have to be the heavy hammer,'" *New York Post*, July 15, 2023.

Land, Olivia, "Gilgo Beach suspect Rex Heuermann once stalked employee onto cruise ship: I could find you anywhere," *Newsday*, September 12, 2023.

MacKay, Frank, "The LISK Series," Podcast (ongoing).

Marino, Joe; Larry Celona, Tina Moore, Craig McCarthy and Jack Morphet, "Gilgo 'Serial Killer' Nabbed," *New York Post*, July 15, 2023.

Meko, Hurubie, "Twilight of the Serial Killer: Cases Like Gilgo Beach Became Even Rarer,' *New York Times*, August 6, 2023.

Miller, John and Christina Maxouris, "Investigators in Gilgo Beach Case on Theory that the Killings Occurred in Suspect's Home," *CNN*, July 21. 2023.

Moynihan, Ellen and Josephine Stratman, "The Real People Who Suffered Awful Ends" *Daily News*, July 15, 2023.

Murphy, Mary, "Investigators in NY cold case seek help from Gilgo Homicide Task Force," *PIX11 News*, August 9, 2023.

Namm. Stuart, *A Whistleblower's Lament*, Hellgate Press, 2014.

O'Keeffe, Michael, "Gilgo Beach Killings: Police Say They are Scouring DNA, Seized Materials for Possible Rex Heuermann Link to 6 Unsolved Slayings" *Newsday,* July 20, 2023.

O'Keeffe, Michael and Nicole Fuller, "Former Suffolk Chief of Police James Burke charged with sexual misconduct, officials say," *Newsday*, August 22, 2023.

O'Keeffe, Michael and Nicole Fuller, "Former Suffolk Chief if Police James Burke charged with sexual solicitation," *Newsday*, August 22, 2023.

O'Keeffe, Michael, "2 of 4 charges dropped against James Burke, ex-Suffolk police chief arrested in sex solicitation sting, documents show," *Newsday*, August 29, 2023.

O'Neill, "NY officials probing Gilgo Beach suspect Rex Heuermann in unsolved 1989 murder," New York Post, September 7, 2023.

Palmer, Tom, "Attorney calls wife of accused Gilgo Beach serial killer an accomplice," *News Nation*, August 12, 2023.

Parnaby, Laura, "Gilgo Beach murders suspect Rex Heuermann and disgraced cop who botched investigation may have met 'gay cruising' at one of Long Island's notorious 'Pickle Parks", claims victims' lawyer," *DailyMail,com*, September 3, 2023.

Parpan, Grant, "Gilgo Beach Killings: Suspect Rex Heuermann's defense proposed cheek swab, court filings show," *Newsday,* August 8, 2003.

Parpan, Grant, "Suspect Rex Heuermann must submit to cheek swab for DNA testing, judge rules," *Newsday*, August 9, 2023.

Parpan, Grant," Gilgo Beach Killings: Prosecutors seek to turn over hundreds of Rex Heuermann' s guns to Nassau, court filings say," *Newsday*, September 8, 2023.

Parpan, Grant, "Former Suffolk Police Chief James Burke pleads not guilty to charges of public lewdness, indecent exposure stemming from sex solicitation ring," *Newsday*, September 12, 2023.

Parpan, Grant, "Gilgo Beach killings: Nassau prosecutors probing alleged serial killer Rex Heuermann's seized guns, court filing shows," *Newsday*, October 6, 2023.

Parpan, Grant and Nicole Fuller, "Gilgo Beach killings: Rex Harrison submits to DNA test, sources say," *Newsday*, August 24, 2023.

Poleo Germania Rodriguez, "Gilgo Beach 'serial killer' Rex Heuermann is meeting with clergyman once a week while in jail, as top cop says he's been taken off suicide watch and is emotionless," *DailyMail.com*, August 28, 2023.

Rodriguez, Germania, "Gilgo Beach Serial Killer Suspect Rex Heuermann 'Killed at Least One of his Victims at his Home,'" *DailyMail.com*, July 20, 2023.

Sheehan, Kevin and Jorge Fitz-Gibbon, "Gilgo Beach Suspect Rex Heuermann May Have Killed his Victim in Soundproof Room, Cops Using Cadaver Dogs to Search Yard," *New York Post*, July 23, 2023.

Sisak, Michael, "Prosecutors in Gilgo Beach killings are giving Rex Heuermann's defense a vast trove of evidence" *NBC New York*, August 1, 2023.

Suffolk County District Attorney, Bail Application re Rex A. Heuermann, 2023.

Tillett, Andy and Emily Crane, "The Gilgo Beach Burial Grounds" *New York Post*, July 15, 2023.

Murphy, Mary, "Wife's DNA on the Bodies Found at Gilgo Beach Led to Arrest of Rex Heuermann" PIX 11 News, July 16, 2023.

Offenhartz, Jeff. "Dave Schaller came fact to face with alleged Gilgo Beach serial killer Rex Heuermann; 12 years later, his tip helped crack the case" Associated Press, July 23, 2023.

Patch Staff, "What is Mitochondrial Analysis Used on Accused Gilgo Killer's Pizza" Riverhead Patch, July 18, 2023.

Psycho Neighbor, "Full Timeline leading up to Rex Heuermann's Arrest Years of Murder) Must Watch – Stay Safe" Psycho Neighbor YouTube Channel. August 2023.

Sheehan, Kevin and Jorge Fitz-Gibbon, "Hulking Gilgo suspect Rex Heuermann sports weird hairdo as prosecutors confirm DNA found in pizza links him to victim" *New York Post*, September 27, 2023.

Shell, Mary, "My Boss, the Monster" Intelligencer (online), July 25, 2023.

Spangler, Nicholas, "Ocean Parkway thickets Masked Dumping Ground" *Newsday*, July 29, 2023.

Tracy, Thomas; Emma Siewell and Larry McShane, "Accused Monster Pleads Not Guilty" *Daily News*, July 15, 2023.
Hayden, Michael Edison, "The Strange Rise and Violent Fall of Long Island's Dirtiest Police Chief" *Vice.com*, March 15, 2006.

Wolfe, Elizabeth and Jessica Xing, "Wife of Gilgo Beach serial killings suspect and her attorney open up about the family's experience since Rex Heuermann's arrest" *CNN*, August 1, 1023.

PHOTO CREDITS

Gilgo Beach Bodies, Suffolk County Police Department

James Burke, *CBS News*

Thomas Spota and Christopher McPartland, *Newsday*

Christoper Loeb, *New York Post*

Judge Stuart Namm, Law.com/Rick Kopstein

Johnny Pius, FundaGrave.com. John V.

Thomas Ryan, *Newsday*

Jerry Steuerman, theywillkill.com

Martin Tankleff, Oprah.com

Shannan Gilbert, AP

Joseph Brewer. TrueCrimeResearchers.com

Lieutenant Kevin Beyrer, LinkedIn.com

Gilgo Four, CBS News

Dr. Peter Hackett, MEAWW.COM

Lowrita Rickenbacker, Pinterest.com

Attorney John Ray, soundcloud.com

Suffolk County Executive Steve Bellone, *Newsday*

Former Suffolk County Executive Steven Levy, LinkedIn.com

John Oliva, *Newsday*

Lieutenant James Hickey, Facebook.com

District Attorney Ray Tierney, Former District Attorney Tim Sini, *Newsday*

Senator Phil Boyle, *Long Island Press*

Greg Blass, RiverheadLocal.com

Suffolk County Legislator Robert Trotta, stonybrook.edu

Michael Pak, historyvshollywood.com

James Bissett, libn.com

Joseph James DeAngelo, BBC

Valerie Mack, Phillyvoice.com

Jessica Taylor, Facebook.com

Rita Tangredi, *The New York Times*

Colleen McNamee, *The New York Times*

Sandra Costilla, *Long Island Press*

Attorney William Keahon with Defendant John Bittrolff, *Newsday*

Sgt. Michael Murphy, Suffolk County Police Department

Suffolk County Police Commissioner Rodney Harrison, Suffolk County Police Department

Rex Heuermann, *Newsday*

Rex Heuermann (suit), *New York Post*

Karen Vergata, Facebook.com

Aaliyah Bell, FBI

Julia Ann Bean, *NBC News*

Misty Marie Saens, *DailyMail.com*

Victoria Camera, *News12*

Jodi Marie Brewer, missingandmurdered.co.uk

Lindsay Marie Harris, *Fox News*

Jessica Edith Louise Foster, Reddit

ABOUT THE AUTHOR

Writing Credentials:

Robert Joseph Banfelder is an award-winning crime-thriller novelist as well as an author of true crime. Two of Robert's novels, *The Author* and *The Teacher*, received "Best Suspense Novel" awards from NewBookReviews.org; both are in their second printing (2013). Robert is the recipient of an Achievement Award from *Who's Who in America* (2005); a Lifetime Achievement Award (2017). The author's latter works, titled *The Long Island Serial Killer Murders—Gilgo Beach and Beyond*, followed by its sequel *Snuff Stuff*, are written under the umbrella of New Journalism; that is, a mix of fact and fiction.

Robert's nonfictional treatment of Suffolk County's past law enforcement's Culture of Corruption, dating back to 1979, is riveting—hopefully having ended with the formation of the Gilgo Beach Homicide Investigation Task Force (2022), and the arrest of purported serial killer Rex Andrew Heuermann (2023). Is *R*ex Heuermann the *K*ing of serial killers . . . or your garden variety murderer? Robert examines this question and highlights the ongoing investigation in his latest book titled *The Long-Awaited Arrest of Long Island Serial Killer Rex Heuermann* subtitled *Past Administration to Blame.*

Eighteen (18) books comprise Robert's cannon of literary works [see Roman numerals iii–v at the beginning of this book]. Additionally, he has penned several hundred articles, primarily relating to the great outdoors. They have appeared in national and regional publications such as *The Fisherman*, *On The Water*, *Big Game Fishing Journal*, *Hana Hou! The Magazine for Hawaiian Airlines*, *Deer & Deer Hunting*, *New York Game & Fish*, *Northwoods Sporting Journal*, *GUNS* magazine, to name but a few.

Six of Robert's 'Smart-Series' handbooks include *The Fishing Smart Anywhere Handbook for Salt Water and Fresh Water*; *The North American Small & Big Game Hunting Smart Handbook*; *Bull's Eye! The Smart Bowhunter's Handbook*; *The Essential Guide to Writing Well & Getting Published*; *On Your Way to Gourmet Cooking*; and *Gourmet Cooking with Confidence*. The two cookbook publications are coauthored with Donna Derasmo.

In the latter part of 2023, the *New York Post* interviewed Robert and published an article on his take regarding the **L**ong **I**sland **S**erial **K**iller case. Too, Robert was most recently interviewed for a documentary (which may not be revealed at this point in time) referencing the **LISK** investigation.

Moreover, Robert co-hosts with Donna Derasmo their YouTube Channel titled *Special Interests with Bob & Donna*. The channel is eclectic, covering numerous topics such as true crime, politics, the great outdoors, and gourmet cooking.

Education:

Robert graduated Queens College with a Bachelor of Arts ~ English honors (cum laude). He received his Master of Arts (genre, creative writing), also from Queens College.

Robert taught English Composition at Queensborough Community College, Queens College, Montefiore Community Center, and the

State University of New York (SUNY) at Purchase. Additionally, he designed and taught numerous adult education courses at Queensborough Community College.

A complete listing of Robert's work may be viewed on his extensive website: www.robertbanfelder.com.

Facebook@Robert Banfelder
Twitter@RobertBanfelder

Made in United States
Orlando, FL
25 November 2023

39431843R10095